Charles Chase Lord

Poems of Penacook

Charles Chase Lord

Poems of Penacook

ISBN/EAN: 9783744782890

Printed in Europe, USA, Canada, Australia, Japan

Cover: Foto ©Andreas Hilbeck / pixelio.de

More available books at **www.hansebooks.com**

POEMS

OF

PENACOOK

THE SEER.

PRELUDE.

———

SWEET love, come! The hour is dark;
  Above the path,
  In frowning wrath,
The storm-clouds gather, drifting low;
Thy promise is a tiny spark,
  Thy full effulgence show.

O sweet love, come! The time is long;
  While sorrow weeps,
  The shadow creeps
Too slowly; from enshrouded years,
The world's eternity of wrong,
  Sad thought infers with tears.

O sweet love, come! The day is late;
  Adown the sky
  His footsteps try
The steep, his goal the gloomy west;
Hope tires; impatiently we wait
  Thy endless morning blest.

THE SEER.

THERE is a river,[1] and its current bears
     The sparkling drops that, from the Crystal Hills,[2]
Come trickling down in ceaseless, lustrous flow,
To blend in rills and brooks, that rippling glide
And babbling haste to seek the channel wide,
Where waters many mingle and with zeal,
And rush, and dash, and rout, compete for rest
And rapture in the boundless, shining sea.
Through ever fertile meads of living green,
This river winds, and oft on either hand
Some grander height, adorned with leafy pride,
Invites the eye that dwells on prospects fair ;
While in the bosom of the stream, that glows
With daylight's fervor, lie sweet gems of isles,
The jewel glints of nature's sunlit smile :
And broader, rarer, richer, thus the scene
Compels delight far to the ocean wave.

Upon the surface of this river bright,
One sweeps the oar, or, in its limpid depths,

Seeks zest luxurious in healthful meed,
Or wanders in the meadows, culling blooms,
Or on the farther heights o'erlooks the vale,
To praise its beauty and perchance to tell,
In numbers, wealth, and fame, the busy marts
That owe estate and station to the stream
That e'er submits to bonds of prosy pelf,
Serves labor's end, while tempting art's emprise
In gentler poesy of mystic vein;
Or he, for memories of legends old,
In mind ignores all present toils and cares,
And, taking up the thread of dim events,
That far retreat within the shades of time,
He traces fain the course of stalwart deeds
And startling wonders, wrought in ancient days,
When the great life now surging was unborn,
Till, thought forgetting themes and things that are,
His fancy revels in old dreams that were.

INTERLUDE.

SKY, so beautiful and bright,
    O tell us whence, below, above,
Came we within thy sphere of light—
    So much to see, so much to love—
When morn the sunlit flood unbars,
When eve reveals the moon and stars!

O sun, whose beams adorn the day
   And guide creation's feet aright;
O moon and stars, whose love-lights play
   To cheer the aspects of the night;
What treasures of thy vision hold
The secret of the eons old?

The accents of the morn are dumb,
   The voices of the eve are still:
From man's own lips the word shall come,
   When wisdom all the world shall fill,
With soul and sense, effulgent, bright,
The morning and the evening light.

OFT is a day when clouds obscure the sun
   Of the dark world, and earth in somber weeds
Sits dumb in shade and fosters dim designs
Of dull futurity; but when a ray
Breaks from the blazing dome, a narrow rift
In dismal vapors parting, hope revives
In earth's cold bosom, and a winsome smile
Lights all the face of nature, glad and gay,
For promise yet of sunshine full and free,
When wild and field together shall the prize
And blessing reap in leaf, and bud, and bloom.
The soul of man in shadows likewise droops
When daylight languishes, and love's bright orb,

Lord of the realms ascendant, veils his face
In the dank mists of sense, the wiles of time
Faith's prospects blinding, till the heart of doubt
And dread revives in sparkling, pure delight
For one blest ray that cheers the broad expanse
Of being, sentient of peace and pain,
When clouds roll off and sunshine beams afar:
And, as the wilderness and fruitful land,
In nature's scheme, express their kindred pride,
Both low and high, in life's diviner plan,
Partake of treasure and their sorrows hide.

Three hundred years and fifty,[3]—let us count
In teeming fancy, for uncertain time
Far backward reaches to a home and scene
From which the thread inceptive of this tale,
So oddly told, takes up lithe fancy's course
To fact seen culminative.   In the past—
So dim, so strange to life's conception late!—
When erst the land, through which the river bright
Far seaward courses, was a waste and wild,
Where savage hordes usurped the vast domain,
In a rude shelter, on a lofty hill,[4]
That from the west o'erlooks the eastern vale,
Where winds the stream in motion tortuous,
There dwelt the chief who swayed the local clan
Of instincts rude, in majesty enshrined.

Great Kunnewa,[5] of Nipmuck [6] blood and fame,
Was lord of Penacook,[7] and in his house,
A wigwam wrought of wood, and bark, and skins,[8]
Abode his faithful wife, true, royal squaw,
Whose feats domestic won the pride and praise
Of all her sisters dusky of the tribe.
She planted maize, and beans, and luscious gourds,
And trained their growth, and plucked the harvest rich
In bounty pleasant to life's crude emprise,
But far too small for expectation high
That now pervades the breast of tillage fair.
Yet while she toiled, this wife of Kunnewa,
Newissit [9] named, there oft a silent shade
Crept o'er her face, and then betimes she spoke
Of deep concern for life's swift issues vast,
The while her thought seemed wider than the world:
And then she told how oft her spirit walked
And talked with Manit [10] and his happy host,
And said, "O squaws of braves, Keep ear! Keep eye!
The good Great Spirit haunts the thoughtless world—
Breathes in the corn, and in the blossom smiles,
When bean and gourd rejoice in pleasant light,
And, when the bee the sweet drop sips and sings,
The Spirit's voice exults in gladness free."

One morning Kunnewa, the sachem brave,
Arose to greet the early dawning day,

And forth advance upon the missions bold
That e'er engrossed the fierce and ardent breast
Of savage men that stooped ne'er once to toil.[11]
With tomahawk in belt, his bow he grasped,
His well stocked quiver o'er his shoulder swung,
The nimble deer to capture, or the bear
Of slow yet direful pace to render doom,
Or e'en some foe incautious of his tribe
Compel to bite the dust, for Penacooks
Oft met sharp war in service of the wild.
As Kunnewa, the chief, thus purpose held
In preparation, from her couch of skins
Awoke Newissit, wife and thoughtful squaw,
To look upon her lord, in armor clad,
With features set, his skin in painted hues,
For terror swift and vengeance quick and sure.
The gentle squaw uplooked with startled gaze
And troubled vision, while with hasty words
She spoke her thought in soft but earnest plaint.
"You wake me with your moods," she said in pain,
"And fright my eyes and scare away my dream
Of things too pure and peaceful for the day
That dawns alone for ceaseless war and woe ! "
Then Kunnewa, the sachem, warrior great,
In wonder on his spouse his aspect turned
And said, "What mean ye by this doleful speech
To him who lives to lure and lash his foes,

Until, as dead leaves fly before the breeze,
They sink, and waste, and wander, vanquished, dumb?"
Then answered fair Newissit, "As I lay
Asleep before you waked me by a sound,
I dreamed and saw the shining, distant east,
To which the wigwam opes, and, lo! the sun
Arose in mighty strength, yet shed his light
Upon the world as beams a tender smile:
And, as I looked, behold! a sachem bright
Came from the sun and stood before the door,
His face in sweetness clad, and all his form
Was rich in shapely mould and lustrous mien.
The feathers on his head were sunlit flames,
His mantle fell in folds of daylight sheen,
And, on his feet, the moccasins he wore
With dewdrops sparkled, nameless in their glow.
Thus, while I wondered, yet without a fear,
What mission strange this shining sachem bore,
He spoke,—' I am the Manit, and I come
To tell thee things that yet shall gladly be.
The time is ripe with trouble and with tears,
And angry death the harvest reaps in blood,
But these my people yet shall see a sign.
As the new moon breaks softly in the west,
To fill the night with all its gentle fire,
The new man comes to thoughtless passion sway
And tame the hearts that now in fierceness rage,

And one morn when the sun upon the sky
Seeks his far height above the lustrous world,
Thy soul shall bow, and forth shall come thy child,
Son of the sun, and he shall wisdom find
And truth impart, while, man of medicine,
His wondrous deeds shall fame his name afar.
His heart shall bear the treasure of the sun,
His thought shall know the riches of the moon,
And all the stars shall speak him face to face,
And while the wind shall blow, the waters run,
And leaf and blossom deck the landscape wide,
He shall have skill to teach and guide the tribe
That by his judgment, in rare aspects seen,
Shall many woes escape and gladness find—
In valor proud, so keen his sight shall be.' [12]
As thus he spoke, I waked and lost my dream."

When Kunnewa, the lordly chief, this tale
Had listed fully, once expression strange
His face betokened, and a softer light
Beamed in his features.   Briefly to the eye
Of his fond squaw, it seemed a gentler mien
And nobler joy, in kinder aims fulfilled,
Recast his being in diviner mould,
Disclosing godlike presence in the man.
Upon Newissit once he cast a glance
Beneficent; then on his bow he looked

And touched his quiver with half-careless hand,
As if a sudden thought to lay it by
Had half possessed his soul; and then the strength
Of savage ardor in his breast revived,
His aspect darkened, and his form grew fierce,
The while he made reply,—"The Manit lives,
The Sachem great, who all things makes and rules,
And sun, and moon, and stars his will obey,
And on the storm he rides, and in the light
Smiles on the world, and gives his children bread
Of the green fields and meat of forests dark
And of deep waters; and, some day, at last,
As sunshine breaks for storms, his heart may turn
Our lives from war to peace, and in the earth
Lay low the tomahawk [18] in endless rest:
But till he comes to stay the warlike arm
That draws the bow, and speeds the arrow sharp,
And swings the hatchet high, the foe to kill,
I, Kunnewa, the chief of Penacook,
Will know no rest while other tribes invade
My realm for spoil; and all my trusty braves
I rally to the fight till death for aye."
Thus having said, he forth assumed his way,
His fate to bear and prowess swift attest.

Newissit, from that hour, a sacred pledge
And pleasure fostered in her deepest breast,

And pondered oft upon the Spirit's words;
And, while she tended oft the rising corn,
Or climbing bean, or graceful, roving gourd,
Her rapt reflection strayed in pleasant light
Through fields of joyful hope and promise sweet:
And when, one morn, within her wigwam kind,
She saw the sunbeams break across the vale,
Where wound the river through the verdant meads,
To enter by her door and bless her face,
And heard the cheerful word, " It is a son,"
Her soul, ecstatic, rose in virtue's pride
Till skies seemed near and earth sank far away.
The child grew strong, and as the patient years
Their seasons told, in favor thrived apace,
And oft some eye observant marked the grace
Of mien and mind that flourished in such might
In life so tender and in days so few.
In childish ranks he drew the mimic bow,
And joined the chase pretended, and his zeal
Oft won the prize of boyhood's valor feigned,
And, little chief, he bore the signal plume [14]
In childlike majesty, nor once he deigned
To honor wound or seem of vain conceit
Of lofty privilege for other's pain,
And thus found praise of all, or young, or old:
Yet greater virtue claimed his service true.
Betimes, when comrades of his childhood strove

In tempting sports, he fled the mirthful van
And in seclusion sought some odd recourse
Of childlike fancy, nor his face was seen
Within the daily circle, till his mind,
In secret contemplation in the dell,
Or on the height, some deep conception gained
Of life and law to common natures vain;
And e'er from such excursions of the soul
In silent realms he brought some hint, or art,
Of mind mysterious that probed all things
E'en to their depths, the while he spoke the word,
Or wrought the deed, whose province e'er escapes
All but the great magician, he whose grasp
Of thought and theme all subtle wisdom solves,
And he whose will all plastic nature makes
Subservient; and thoughtful braves beheld
The growing boy and said with solemn mien,
" He makes his medicine,[15] and yet will be
A mighty chief of wonders seen and known."
Such things Newisset cherished, and her heart
Grew big with expectation, while she watched
Her darling boy in manly grace increased,
Each day her hope's fulfillment, as the lad
Leaned on her breast in filial love's return
For love maternal, till fruition rich
Once thrilled her soul and made existence blest
In bright reality.   One autumn eve,

Within the wigwam's shelter, while she⁻sat,
To look beyond the door and see the vale,
Resplendent in the moonlight soft and full,
She felt a hand upon her shoulder laid
And gladdened, for her son, the well-beloved,
Close to her side, withdrawn from outward scenes,
Approached her tenderly and touched her form
In potent phase of blessing; and, her heart
In pride exultant, of light thought, she said,
"Whence come ye?" Then he said, with strange con-
　　cern
And odd emprise of fervor, " From the play
Wherein I saw a vision, great and true,
Although no other lad in sport was keen
To see the wonder, and I come to tell
Your ear and loose my troubled heart in bonds
Of startled care and fear unfelt before."
Then she responded, "Tell me all, my child!
The Spirit, the Great Manit, walks the world,
And oft his presence prompts the restless eye
To see his face and form, or mark the signs
By which he turns the thought to purer themes
And deeper knowledge.   Let your heart be calm!"
Then he, with ardor, though in quiet, broke
His burdened mind and thus his vision told:
" But just a space ago, when, with the boys,
I played the deer and wolf [16] upon the green,

The moon, big with the harvest, up the east
Came shining, as you now in full behold
It only smaller, and we stopped in play
To look upon its face, so wide and round,
And then I saw the wonder.   From the moon,
Came forth great, dark canoes, as on the sea,
With wings of white, and touched the solid land,
And from them poured armed hosts of paleface braves,
And some on horses, and great guns they drew
That seemed to flash and thunder like the cloud
That bursts upon the sky when the sharp heat
Has scorched the earth and made the light leaves droop
Upon the thrifty tree : and, as I looked,
A paleface powwow,[17] in a blanket long
And dark, his bare head white with flowing locks,
And stepping on before the hasting braves,
He high within his hand upheld a form
Like wide, white leaves together held in bond,
And cried, ' Peace ! Peace !' in speech that made me glad
And then the stars that first began to peep
Seemed nodding to his word, as if he spoke
Great wisdom.   Just then once my lifted hand
I pointed to the moon and with loud voice
Cried out, ' See ! See ! The great canoes ! The braves !
The paleface powwow ! '   Then the laughing boys,
With mocking tongues, made merry ; and I looked
Once more, and all the vision strange had fled."
    2

The mother's heart, when thronged with mystic hopes,
Exults with thrilling rapture when the pledge
Of golden promise in her offspring sweet
Thrives to perfection by the gift of grace
She holds beneficent, supreme, divine.
Newissit listened to the spectral tale
Of her fond son and felt the magic glow
That warms affection into flaming bliss
For treasure rarer found than earth can show
When unillumined by great Heaven's sun,
Serene and holy; and her comfort vast
She spoke unto her child and gave him rest
Of restless yearning for the cause that probed
His being and composure roused to pain :
And when soft, soothing sleep its curtain drew,
Two souls sailed sweetly on the sighless sea.

INTERLUDE.

M Y soul was rapt just now; the passing hour
    Held one blest moment; in a field of light
  I stood; at once I saw a smiling bower,
      With lustrous bloom, that perfume breathed, bedight.

  Close by, within a graceful, spreading tree,
      A trill of bird notes warbled; life was gay;
  A squirrel leaped and chirped in playful glee;
      A sprightly bee tuned for the gladsome day.

The soft air, floating 'neath the crystal sky,
　Lisped gentle melody in leaf and bough ;
A rippling, sparkling brook sang lullaby
　To care, and said, "Heart, heart, be happy now !"

Such transport, brief and blissful !　Thrilled, intense,
　Yet more serene, I deemed earth's sorrows dead ;
Then, as a flame dissolves, the evidence
　Of sweet enchantment shimmered and had fled.

What was it?　Only just a waking dream
　That decked the world with blessing, full and free ;
In subtle mood, reflection cast a gleam
　On one who thinks of, loves, and lives for me.

THE circuit of the sun, in potent light
　And thrilling fervor, oft the world awakes
From wintry stupor and the earth inspires
With spring's lithe energy.　The landscape thrives,
The buds expand, the leaves exult in green,
And blossoms revel in their nameless pride,
And all things triumph in the shining march
To rich maturity that crowns the scene.
Thus from the dark prenatal springs the man,
And, in the gifts and graces loaned of Life,
Creative, boundless, endless, takes his way
To manhood's goal with joy, and glories there
In strength and grandeur, king and lord of all

That, 'neath the sunlit sky, exists and breathes.
The hero of this tale, with hasting time,
His hope accomplished, clad in signal guise
Of man preëminent, majestic, great,
The wisdom and the wonder of his tribe,
And, in succession of the changeless law,
A sachem stood, of royal rank renówned.
Great Kunnewa, his sire, as falls the oak
Before the tempest's blast, by death's fell hand,
Lay prostrate, while the wild, weird, wailing chant
Of faithful braves his spirit buoyed in peace
And wafted gently to the hunting grounds,
Where happy souls no longer grieve nor tire;
And he, true son, who took the regal reign
By right inheritance, of custom bore
His choice cognomen, *Passaconnaway*,
Child of the Bear,[18] and homage claimed and won.

There are of men who bear compounded worth
In matchless measure.   He whose fame we keep,
Chief Passaconnaway, of talents wide,
In fruitful range of useful aims and ends,
In one quick soul a thousand virtues held,
And puissant made all, and blessed his kind.
Nor, in evolving thought, may justice waive
His praise domestic.   Longing, luring love,
Through presents rich and honors bending low,

Had won Sumana,[19] rarest bride and leal,
And to his wigwam brought, and, ripe reward
Of chaste devotion, sons and daughters, found,
Sweet offspring, brave and fair, a father's joy
And mother's swift delight, rare, rich, and pure.
Of noble children, Nanamocomuck
Became the chief Wachusett, and the mild,
Wise Wonalancet, in full time's decree,
His sire succeeded, chief of Penacooks,
And brave Unanunquosit, and the lithe,
True Nonatomecut, unsullied fame
Kept constant, while a daughter, choice and fair,
Wife of brave Nobhow in the course of days,
And bright Wanuchus, she who Saugus loved,
To stir romance that yet thrives in the song
Of the sweet minstrel,[20] proved the worth and praise
Of their great line ancestral.   Lord of realms
That stretched far by the river, of this tale
The theme inceptive, swift,[21] bright Merrimack,
The sachem Passaconnaway his seat
Of royal pride at Namoskeag[22] held fast,
Though oft his zeal of change, in fair emprise
Of pleasure and of patience, fain induced
Transition comforting.   The sachem proud,
In choice diversified—as ever turns
The soul of weighty cares to scenes that soothe
By variation all the thought o'erworn—

For kind and calm composure of the mind,
Loosed free of bonds that chafe and vex the man
Of deep concern for self and subjects true—
Himself in honor conscious of his trust
And strict account to law, unswerving, just,
And endless fondly turned and dwelt apart—
On the fair isle[23] that, northward, in the stream,
Encircled by the water, smiles in light,
Gem of the Merrimack ; or yet he took
His pleasant journey southward on the wave,
Through smiling meadows—cheering thoughts' emprise
Of dark anxiety—till where an isle
Decks the fair river's bosom, ere the stream,
Souhegan called, pours out its flood of toil
And to the Merrimack its task resigns
In the great world hydraulic,[24] there to pause
In grateful pastime.   Nor was he, the chief,
The mighty sachem, found of idle zest
The careless victim, for he wisely sought
The refuge of the isles in spring's bright hours,
To mark the hopeful seed that, dropped to earth,
The promise bore of harvest ripe and rich,
And, through the simple service of the soil,
Suppress the strain that strove with inward stress.

Behold the man, the chief, the sachem wise
To rule his realm with right and reap reward

Of honest homage from his subject tribe,
Yet found of adoration, strange but strong,
For the great marvel of his land and line ;
For he, brave Passaconnaway, had proved
In meed the promise of the Manit, made
To rapt Newissit in the dream of morn,
And, like the Man of twofold nature, viewed
The scenes of time with hints ideal, weird,
That craved exemption of the bonds of sense,
In exaltation of the life that tries
Sublimest heights and shames the world unborn
To rich realities that crown the zeal
Of the quick spirit.   In a savage mien,
Chief Passaconnaway, in cruder phase,
The soul made manifest, and knowledge gained,
And prescience took, of grander force and fact
That far escape the common conscience, set
Too much on earth and earthly aims and ends.[25]
In ways domestic e'er he sought the price
Of simple virtue, and in regal paths
The prize of duty plain allured his eye ;
And, man of medicine, in measure rare,
He touched all hearts and proved his mission deep
In depths mysterious to thoughtless minds
That foster sense and seeming, barren, blind.
The rude, wild tribe, that judgment lacked, in vain
Tried explanation of its sachem's gift

And grace of manhood in transcendent might,
And gave its thoughts to fancy till it dreamed
How he could water burn, the rocks command
To change their stations, and the trees entice
To merry dances, and the live, green leaf
Evolve from ashes of the dry leaf burned,
And make the dead snake's skin writhe yet again,
In life resuscitate, and cold ice show
Upon the surface of the full bowl, hot
With summer's fervor in its liquid depths:
And wilder still swift frenzy raged in flight.
A famed tradition bore the strange report
That once upon the green and happy shore
Of the great lake, the Spirit's joyful smile,[26]
That rare New Hampshire's scenes adorns with pride,
A contest proved great Passaconnaway
Of skill to dare and doom to death with speed
A rival chief, with mystic art endowed,
A challenge tested.   Sitting face to face
Upon the ground, each man his wisdom tried
In emulation; and the greater chief,
Impatient of the trial, all his might
Of medicine assumed, and to his foe,
Of equal skill first found, cried loudly, "Die!"
Then he, the vanquished, sighed, and swayed, and fell,
His spirit parting from the prostrate clay
And floating, homeless, on the mindless wind.

Rude, wild imagination of the tribe,
Of savage thought and instinct, clad the chief
In robes of lurid light that magic weaves
For mindless mortals; but the man within,
To virtue moulded, and to wisdom moved,
And unto strength exerted, proved the aims
That soar above delusion, rash and vain,
And to life's clearer vision, peering high
Above the clouds of sense, reveal the worth,
Serene and bright, sublime and well refined,—
The majesty of selfhood, godlike, great.

INTERLUDE.

I HEED not beauty of the face,
With all the complements of grace,
That admiration win apace,
  Yet thou art very fair, my love;
To all sweet excellence implies
In mould and mien, I close mine eyes;
My hope on other pride relies
  That dwells within thy form, my love.

Bright wealth of thought, transcending sense
With truth's sublimer evidence,
Charms not to lure me in suspense,
  Though thou art very wise, my love;

Than lustrous gems of wisdom's skill,
That nobler adoration fill,
I prize a richer treasure still
   That gleams within thy mind, my love.

For worth that sacred aims reveal,
The heart that craves a purer zeal
Affects me not with swift appeal,
   Yet thou art very good, my love;
Beyond the purpose of thy days,
That guides thy feet in holy ways,
Devotion truer still I praise
   That flames within thy soul, my love.

By fate entranced, I am as he
Who thee beholds and yet to see
A rarer self evolve in thee,
   Though fair, and wise, and good, my love;
Like a rapt vision of the night,
A transport strange refines my sight, —
Thou art transfigured in the light
   That shows thee all divine, my love.

THERE is an instinct true in riper souls
   That far o'erleaps the narrow bounds of self
And widely roams in realms of use, and takes
Of each concern of men an ample meed,
And, in the frame composite of a whole,

Mad chaos tames and order renders mild,
Beneficent, and true, and heals the world.
In civil sway, this spring of nobler law,
In cognizance of broader ends and weal,
Enlists, inlocks, and binds the aims diverse
Of social energy, and man to man
Makes leal and gentle, hopeful, helpful, kind,
Till each, upholding each, makes stable all.
The sachem wise, great Passaconnaway,
Of Penacook the royal head and pride,
In phase eccentric, in the savage realms,
Law's higher rule attested, till he made
War peace, loss gain, and weakness strength,
And saved the heritage of name and fame
Of Penacooks held choice, their ancient line
Esteeming, while their prospects rich and rare,
In schemes participant of others' zest
And worth, involved an intermingled pride
And faith of tribe to tribe with pledges fast.

Chief Passaconnaway, his royal mind
Big with the legends of the warlike days
Known to his fathers—and in childhood's ear
Rehearsed, the swift alternate zest and pain,
For vanquished foe or victor friend, the face
In flush and paleness showing—wisely bent
On firm security of future years,

Seen glad and boonful with prophetic eye,
His brother sachems sought with potent zeal
And speech persuasive, and he broke his thought :
" Ye know, my brothers, how in other days,
My fathers met the foe, the Tarrantine,[27]
Child of the east, with false and cruel breast,
Or yet the Mohog,[28] from the sunset land,
So fierce and bold, with heart to strike with dread,
And bore his anger, while their souls were tried
To stay his march and save the darling lives
Of wives so dear and tender children sweet.
Ye know one year the Mohog came with strength
And pressed our people till, upon the height,[29]
That from the east o'erlooks the Merrimack,
The happy stream through smiling meads that winds,
We built a mighty fort, of fallen trees,
And in it put our wives and children safe,
With fruitful bounties of the earth at hand,
And kept our lives and watched the haughty foe,
His fortress strong upon the farther side
Of the bright river.[30]   Ye have heard us tell
How one sad day, the Mohog, shrewd and bold,
With heart deceitful, sent a daring brave
Across the stream to north, to wander down
E'en to our fort and, by his loneness, seem
Our easy captive ; but, with thoughtless zeal
As we him sought for prize, he wildly fled

And into ambush deadly led us on ;
And though with valor we the battle held,
And to the Mohog gave great bloody woe,
So that e'er since the vexer is no more,
Yet we in weakness drooped till all our pride,
As a lone tree before the tempest bows
And trembles for its fate, in sore fear shakes
Lest some misfortune blast it.   Hear ye now !
What tribe holds safety sure, when, long and lone,
It bears a hostile purpose?   Let us join
Our willing hands, and with our hands our hearts,
Our aims unite, our ends compound in one,
And shame our foes !   The thrifty, clustered wood,
Upon the hilltop bleak, the storm withstands,
And many tribes as one receive the shock
That, harmless unto all, one lone destroys.
Join ye with me !   The future holds our peace
In present prospect.   In my heart I feel
A happy promise, and I see the years
Break from the sun in fertile, fruitful days,
While the moon smiles upon the silent world
In safety sleeping, and the watchful stars
Blink blissfully and bless the balmy scene.
Stay not !   I bear upon my pleading tongue
The message of the Manit, for he breathes
His word upon the air that in my ear
Breaks softly, and his faithful promise smiles

In the green fields, with waving bloom, and glows
In the rich autumn, when the corn is ripe,
And the glad squaws the harvest reap with songs,
And the broad land no solace seeks for tears."

The music of his speech the tribes allured.
And Passaconnaway, the sachem true,
Had fruitage of his labors, and they said
Who listened to his pleading, full of zeal,—
" He has good tongue and speaks the honest word,
And let us join our hands and be his friends,
And keep our lives, and give our wives great peace
And children safety."   Then the pledges fast
They gave with ardor till of tribes of braves
Wise Penacook,[31] and shrewd Pentucket,[32] quick
To see the object prudent, Swamscot,[33] clear
In judgment, Newichwannock,[34] swift to grasp
The thought far reaching—each with each in all—
Made law confederate, and still the clans
Their cause made common, and, for surer ends
Of loyalty and grandeur, him made head—
The chief of chiefs—who wrought the mighty change,
To be Bashaba, prince, supreme, renowned,[35]
While all the land rejoiced, with hush of war,
And smiling bounties of the fertile fields,
And thriving products of the woods and streams,
Till earth seemed proud and life the bliss of dreams.

INTERLUDE.

ANON and ever comes a happy spell
 That halts the dead march of the mournful years,
When sprightly joys time's solemn steps compel,
 And smiles assume the place usurped by tears.

Then budding youth exults in boundless pride,
 With garlands decked, and in the sunlight plays,
And sere and russet age makes haste to hide
 Its weeds, to hail and keep the day of days.

Pale desolation walks with rueful mien
 The earth, while grief demands men's homage meet,
Till oft love's angel from the glad unseen
 Stops thwart the way with mission firm as sweet.

THERE is an hour that oft the lives of men
 Crowns with blest honor, though the shining prize
Of earth's swift emulation in the strife
Of souls ambitious, fails to woo and win
The hearts expectant; and betimes the zeal
That once burns fiercely for time's treasure fair
In sudden aspect turns and flames for worth
That lures, and lasts, and lives for aye and aye,
Forgetting e'er the promise held in trust
But of the glozing world: and happy he

Who, born for wider aims and broader ends,
In gifts surpassing minds of simpler mould,
Turns from the less award and lends his gaze
Straight to the greater, and with ardent zest
Divines the prospect rich and presses on
To ripe fulfillment in the nobler sphere
Of endless virtue.   Passaconnaway,
The grand Bashaba, chieftain, skillful, keen
In thought percipient, of mystic hints
Of soul pervading substance, and of sight
That peeped beyond the veil of time's dark bound,
In mien majestic, such as savage life,
In simple form and phase, on man bestows,
Earth's pride resigned and pleasure sought and found
In deeds of virtue rare, and friend and foe,
Moved by his goodness ripe and wisdom swift,
Thrilled, awed, astonished, for such prescience was
Within his ken as ever fosters fame.

Time lives, and lasts, and ever proves the ends
That oft the feet of men to paths unsought
Divert, direct, compel, till wondrous change
Dawns on the prospects of this life intense
And fraught with issues mighty in their scope
And empire : and betimes a gifted soul
A glimpse anticipant of coming days
In clearness sees, as ever oft the sun

Foretells his march triumphant up the east
By golden luster of the rising morn,
Or ever yet the mild, complacent moon
Sends forth her heralds in pellucid rays
Of silver light, to break the faithful word
That proves her advent on the evening fair.
The time drew nigh when civil law should sway
The land where savage rule in part but held
Earth's destiny, evolving unto wish,
And wealth, and worth transcending ever far
The instinct barbarous, till he who fain
Brooks all its onset strives but to be crushed
Beneath its wheel, resistless, tireless, swift.
Wise Passaconnaway, the sachem true
And great Bashaba, in the social east,
Saw the strong twilight of the civil sun,
Lord of ascending day, and, for pale doubt,
His soul assumed bright truth and humbly bowed,
And homage rendered unto fruitful fact
And deed submissive, pattern of his tribes.[36]
At length, on mission to the distant sea,
Where great Piscataqua its flood combines
And mixes e'er with ocean,[87] once he grasped—
Chief Passaconnaway—the potent hand
Of civil order, and its face, and form,
And mien in contemplation held and viewed
With wonder vast and deep, consuming awe,

3

And in prompt resolution shaped his will
And purpose, just, discreet, exact, and kind.[38]
Then, to his tribes returning, in the stress
Of thought considerate and ardor full,
He spoke the words that from his burning zeal
Broke forth like flashes of a signal fire
In far extended warning. " Hear, my braves ! "
He made his strong appeal. "The tempest swift
Of the Great Spirit sweeps the feeble earth
And proves all things resistless. In its might,
The Manit's torrent from the mountain breaks,
And naught withstands it. Mighty chiefs, and braves
Of valor high, nor strength nor work obtains
When the Almighty Sachem forth extends
His hand unto his purpose. Be ye ware !
The paleface comes, the tempest of the time
And torrent of the season, e'er to bear
On and still on the will, the wish, and wrath
Of the Great Spirit, if a hand but dare
Rise to resist, in ruth and rancor rude
Of rash revenge. Then let the tomahawk
Lie useless, buried in the fertile ground,
The while we smoke the cheerful pipe of peace[39]
Beneath the lisping trees, where soft winds blow;
And let him have our hearts—the Chief that rules
Our fates and days—and in his happy smile,
That lights his face to see our homage sure,

Repose and save the life that e'er we waste
Who strive to stay the future.   In such zeal
Of noble efforts, we may find the way
And learn the wisdom that safe counsel take
Of the hereafter till, our fears allayed,
Our faith confirmed, our courage fortified,
We may abide, and thrive, and care resign ! "
Then while he spoke, the great Bashaba, he
Of soul sincere as e'en of thoughtful mind,
His word made faithful in the action prompt
That doubt dispelled and proved the deed sublime.
To prudent acts and counsels wise disposed,
In judgment keen of aim and end discreet,
In justice sound, he held for friend and foe
The equal measure of the sure reward
And certain penalty in practice true,
And law made eminent in right and rule.
One day, as ever nearer drew and thrived
The mission of the paleface, skilled and strong,
A stranger of the east with wares and words
That ever tempt the eye and charm the ear,
Within the savage circle all his wealth
And art displayed and craved attention kind
And patronage replete with pleasant gain :
And when a redman, doubtful, hasty, rash,
The proffer fair despised and, in his zest
Impassioned, with his weapon sharp and swift,

The life made forfeit of the mercer mild,
The dire, disastrous deed his own made pledge
Of pain and peril.   Passaconnaway
The culprit seized and of his victim's law
His fate made consequent, and to the hand
Of English justice stern the wretch consigned.[40]

There is a sentiment in human souls
That e'er regards the worth that springs from zeal
That halts not at the door of fate that craves
Devotion's sacrifice of self in sooth
And sincere service of the cause it claims
In high supremacy of lofty praise.
The man impetuous who clamors oft
For some preëminence in scheme or skill,
That bears some promise to a wishful world,
And in his soul grieves not, nor bleeds within
His deepest heart, for woe that works its wealth
Of wisdom weighty in the conscience true,
Has no impartment of life's treasures rare,
Rich, and redundant in unending gain.
The great Bashaba, Passaconnaway,
In purpose just and strict example true,
His faith made fact in humble zeal that bore
Its fruit of patience in the face of pain,
That with its dart his bosom probed with smart,
His shrouded soul in sorrow.   Thus was he

A guide revealed in grandeur, chief sublime.
In the rude days, when simple savage clans
And civil circles crude, on shores involved
In claims disputed and in war's alarms,
Wild apprehension oft left rest unfound
Of swift suspicion, thoughtless, senseless, wrong:
And once wise Passaconnaway, the man
Of just discernment and of purpose kind,
When misconception sped to reckless deeds,
Was victim sought of English bold emprise
And rash revenge.   With arms and mission stern,
Of paleface warriors, forty, each with lust
Of causeless blame and booty, came with speed,
To straight fulfill the legal, high behest,
And Passaconnaway, imagined foe,
Seize and make captive in degrading bonds,
For English safety: but, in sequence strange,
A mighty storm and dark Bashaba gave,
Within his distant wigwam, sure escape
From molestation ; yet his woe was deep.
The paleface mission, warlike, rash, and rude,
And mindless of presumption, finding not
The chief of chiefs, with speed surprised and bound
His own true son, brave Wonalancet, trained
To ends discreet and aims of kind intent
By his wise father, and with him indeed
Was bound his gentle squaw, of guileless heart,

And with them both the child of tender years,
A hopeful son and fair, who knew no harm
That bore a purpose baneful unto aught
Of human mould; and, clad in dismal plight,
Such captives hastened to uncertain doom.
Then Passaconnaway, the injured sire
Of a loved household, he who sought but good
For those who gave him pain and tried his soul,
Though master of a host of vengeful braves,
In prudence bore resentment.   Mindful e'er
Of gross injustice, he the nobler code
Of right attested.   Royal chief of tribes,
He straight his charge preferred, and justice urged,
And reparation claimed, until his words,
In perseverance strong, had shown his cause
Triumphant; and his own he took again
To his full heart, and blessed, with pride and tears.[41]

The world of purpose strict and action prompt
Evinces e'er the force concentric, swift
To prove the worth that dwells within a soul
Whose will, and thought, and energy combine
In phase and fact inseparate, the man
In singleness intrenched in virtue strong,
And sure, and sapient of ends complete
And competent in wisdom's sphere and range.
Great Passaconnaway, the chief of chiefs,

In contemplation of the measures vast,
Urged by the Spirit of the boundless world,
Within his scheme to hold the paleface prince
And promise of the days yet kept in store
For his rude, simple children of the wild,
The prospect owned, and to his hope gave pledge
Of his whole being; and, with honest heart,
And humble mind, and words of import wise,
Low at the feet of English prestige proud,
He cast the burden of his keen concern
And thus made suppliance with earnest mien:
"I come, Chief Winthrop, from the savage wild,
Where the wolf howls, the eagle screams, and earth
In fear and startled air e'er yield the voice
Of fierce destruction wasting. . In my tribes,
That thrill with madness, of resentment bred
In their fierce haunts, the flame exulting burns
Of the destroyer. I have seen how he,
The wise Great Spirit of the world so wide,
To you gives knowledge and the skill that proves
Of life the greater safety, though ye raise
The hand that strikes the harder, when ye turn
Your face upon your foes and battle make
So ripe with death and deep with flowing blood.
I come, O paleface chief, as one who looks
Across the boundless sea, when for the sun
Of happy morn he waits, the light to shine

On his dark path and show the homeward way
To rest and comfort of his soul that tires.
Take me and mine, and in your purpose vast
Let us have part, that we may life preserve
And plenty find, the while we learn and prove
That all our good is yours, as rivers run
Together till their waters poured in one
Rush with resistless speed to find the sea,
And in the deep, wide ocean live for aye.
I speak to you and all my sons through me
Speak as I do: then give us all your heart!" [42]

In mission wise, sincere, and firm emprise,
The great Bashaba of his zeal found grace,
Reward, and peace, and in his sovran state,
Of English law the subject, lived and thrived.

INTERLUDE.

THIS is my offering; my breast,
 Its zeal surcharged, invoked some art,
 Blithe offspring of a transport blest,
  But thou hast touched and tried my heart.

With ceaseless throbbing of the brain,
 Its thought too vast, of mission kind,
My instincts craved a glad refrain,
  But thou hast probed and plagued my mind.

Sweet presence troubling! This my lay,
 Its theme so swift yet half unsung,
A voice besought of accents gay,
 But thou hast foiled and filched my tongue.

Thus shall my rapture droop and faint,
 Its glow all pale, for grief has stole
My joy, and loss will weave its plaint
 Till thou hast loved and loosed my soul.

THE thought of prudent man embraces skill
 Of aim and action in the sphere of life
That mundane welfare fosters, and it guides
The footsteps of lithe progress to the goal
Of expectation fair in triumph just
And joyful, till the land in measure rich
Finds safety, wealth, and honor : yet there spring
From depths of yearning in the human breast
The needs, the wants, the crying wishes swift,
That plead—for exigencies timeless, vast
In soulful scope—the boundless worth and work
That soothes deep sorrow's heart and, faithful, proves
The wisdom of this transient, glozing world
But foolishness—so poor, so weak, so vain!
Anon and e'er some man of mighty strength
In earth's oft counsels of the hour and end,
Auspicious or portentous, zest and zeal,

In contemplation of some aspect grave
Of dread futurity, in feeblest state
Lays down.   The chief, great Passaconnaway,
Of instincts common unto flesh and blood,
But human in the function of a man,
This truth found evident and lent his soul
To search for wisdom of the world unwon.
One day, this wise Bashaba, subject true
Of English royalty in safer rule,
Met a great wonder.   To his ear had come
The oft repeated fame of him who bore
The message of a Monarch, greater still
Than earth's chief potentate, while on his lips
Dwelt fate unchangeable, for he was son
And servant of his Lord and Master, high
In majesty resistless, endless, fierce :
And Passaconnaway the import held
In consternation, lest, a powwow, rare
And ruthless, vengeance taking sure and swift
Of mighty medicine on rival foes
Presumptuous, drew near to strike with doom
And death despairing, and seclusion sought
And trembled, yet his better, unseen lot
Awaited.   In time's full and fair decree,
On mission at Pentucket, face to face,
He gazed upon the emissary strange
Of a still stranger Chief—and looked in vain

To see his weapons sharp, and felt no mist
Of dullness o'er his startled senses steal,
And, for expected darkling wrath, his face
Beheld benign, while, through its tender smiles,
Broke words of gentleness, assuring, sweet,
For speech anticipated harsh with scorn,
And grasped his hand, unmoved in action dire
To aught directed—and his spirit thrilled,
Astonished that such worth in high emprise
Should mien so lowly bear and life so meek.[43]

Suns rose and fell, moons waxed amain and waned,
A year fulfilled its course and told complete
Its tale of varied seasons and the change
That ever life holds subject, and the mind
Of Passaconnaway, of musing thought
In deeper contemplation, dwelt within
On hasting days and time's approaching goal
Of swift transition to the unseen realm
Of the hereafter, till he inly craved
Some full assurance of some entrance fair
Within some sphere of spirit, soul and sense
In strict integrity, when present scenes
Had vanished, and the past had laid in store
All their fond excellence and treasure dear,
Shorn of their future prospects e'er and aye :
And thinking thus his soul found cheerful light

And pleasant comfort.   While again he sought
Some end of regal service to his tribes,
He southward journeyed, and the stranger rare—
The paleface powwow high, and yet so low
In his demeanor—once again his soul
Accosted, and his hand put forth in peace
And pledge of friendship, and an ear besought
For speech of consolation for time's woes,
And life's dull doubts, and fears that ever haunt
Reflection mindless of eternal hopes
And endless joys that of God's goodness take
Their sure fruition ; and Bashaba, chief
Of mighty savage sway, and skilled in lore
Of wisdom barbarous, sat lowly down,
And with his chosen braves of counsel true,
In silence listened, and the powwow pale,
The pious Eliot, apostle sent ·
Of Lord Messiah, thus his message gave :

"Dear brothers of the wild, I here uphold
The Word Omnipotent.   He whom I serve—
The Lord from Everlasting—bids me speak
Your peace and profit, for, the time at hand
Of his approaching kingdom, ye have need
Of his blest comfort of the life that is,
And that which is to come, when death shall close
Your present pilgrimage on time's bleak shores.

Within my hand behold the pledge he gives—
The Lord Almighty—of his holy will
And wish complacent to his children dear,
Of whom are we, created by his hand,
And, by his bounty of the land and sea,
Preserved from day to day and fitly framed
For his true service. Let me read, I pray,
From this—the Holy Book, his own true word—
That ye may know his counsel. Thus he says :
From the bright rising of the eastern sun
Until its going down to western dark,
My name shall mighty be among the tribes—
The scattered Indians, and in each place
Shall honored be with prayer full oft and pure ;
For great my name shall be, saith he, the Lord
Of hosts, among the Indians.[44] To you
Comes such announcement. May ye rightly mark
Its potent meaning ! As the sun that burns
In the blue sky with sweeping luster lights
Earth's farthest bound, the truth of God, my Chief,
Shall fill the world till each dear child he owns
Shall know his right to rule and of his grace
Have sweet cognition. Of his promise vast,
Are ye partakers. Keep your hearts in faith
And holy pleasure ! Yet be doubly ware
How ye esteem his favor ! He, the Lord,
Seeks no vain homage of the world in pride,

But, in soft penitence for evil done,
And in the service of good deeds to come,
He will have sacrifice of self and sin
To win his face and prove his love benign.
So take ye heed, my brothers, how ye bear
His Name in honor, for it is a Name
Not given to our flesh, but, treasure deep,
Cast in our spirits, and which no one knows
Save he who, it receiving, glows within
With righteous fervor of the law fulfilled
In his own nature, as for aye one feels
His own heart beat and thus the fact divines
Of his own being.   This, God's holy Name,
Once stablished in our souls, each heart remoulds
And forms the likeness of his own till love,
Warm and divine, replaces earth's cold hate,
And, by the inward working of his will
In man thus vivified, renews, exalts,
And perfects all the being for the day
Of our redemption, when, from sin escaped,
And in the full exemption of the life
Immortal, holy, happy, we shall stand
Unblemished in God's sight, the image each
Of his bright Son triumphant, of his right
And worth eternal richly to partake
In glory everlasting.   Wherefore, I,
His servant undeserving, ye beseech

To hearken well and heed the message sure,
And, putting off the filthy robes of guilt,
Put on the robe of righteousness unfeigned,
And, watchful unto faith, confess and pray
To him with zeal unceasing, that he may
On each bestow the Name above all names
Which he ordains to be, and to be held
In veneration, till each knee shall bow
And every tongue confess its fame supreme
From the far east e'en to the distant west
Of this the boundless world, while from below
Up to his throne exalted in the skies
The proclamation of its honor swells.
So may ye find escape in God's great day
Which, now appointed, shall in perfect light
Reveal the secret heart and purpose deep
Of each before him summoned, and when he
Shall judge his children by the standard true
Of him who, Man and God, presents the type
Of our salvation ; and the hapless soul
That thrives not with the Name above all names
Shall desolation find and dark despair,
Cut off among its people,—from which end
May God preserve ye ! Hear ye, and heed how ! "

Thus spoke the paleface powwow, while his voice
Rose high in exhortation, and his words

In supplication strong, for the quick sign
Of their complacency of heart and mind
Who listened ; and chief Passaconnaway
And his wild braves, with solemn faces, heard
The great monition, silent, thoughtful, stern.
Then he, Bashaba wise, his soul awaked
To contemplation of life's nobler theme,
In honest speech responded : " All your words,
O powwow of the Chief that rules the world,
Come to my ear with good, and yet a new
And strange thought in them to my soul reveals
A wondrous meaning. From the early morn
Of these, my days, when childhood roamed and
    played,
Till now when I behold my noonday sun
Glide to the west, I e'er have known and served
The wise Great Spirit of my ancient sires,
And of his word, well spoken to my mind,
Have much direction found to soothe and cheer
The prospect of life's journey. Yet withal
Have I much care felt oft, and in my soul
Seemed looking out as to some region vast,
And far away across some ocean wide,
Where rests the spirit of the brave that tires
Of ceaseless tossing on life's restless waves
Within its slight canoe, that floats and still
E'er threatens soon to sink in blackness deep

And hopeless,—though I never yet to pray
Have once found purpose. But your words so strange,
That crave the heart made new by worth within,
To work alone the peace that lives and lasts
In presence of the Manit, who will judge
All work at last, move me indeed to pray
And seek his favor : and my sons shall hear
My thought and of its sure intent receive
My counsel to observe and well pursue
The prompt example.   So may we indeed
Have wisdom unto good for aye and aye !
Great friend, receive my promise and be sure
Of my true tongue, and be you swift to come
And dwell among us, so our lives may learn
Of your direction in the path of right ;
And that, within our midst, you oft may pray
To the Great Spirit that no direful woes
Such as you speak for those who heed not him
Who gives the Name above all other names
Shall come upon us.   Speaking, I have done."

INTERLUDE.

THE thought flies east, the thought flies west,
   The land is broad where treasures be,
But the heart still longs for a portion blest
      Over the silent sea.

A song breathes high, a song breathes low,
   Sweet music charms with varied key,
But the ear still lists where the zephyrs blow
    Over the silent sea.

The light gleams bright, the light gleams soft,
   Rich, blended hues adorn the lea,
But the eye still peers for a luster oft
    Over the silent sea.

The time gives work, the time gives rest,
   Diversion just tempts care to flee,
But the soul still dreams of a boon expressed
    Over the silent sea.

O life doth wound! O life doth heal!
   Conserving law binds you and me,
But a love still yearns, as its fancies steal
    Over the silent sea.

THE bright sun lights the passive world in pride,
  But sinks and seeks the west to darkness own;
The lustrous moon illumes the sphere of night
To drop and disappear, its lamp burned low;
The greater stars and lesser, one by one,
The shaded dome embellish with their glints
Of cheerful radiance, and then they glide
E'en to their setting, and their feebler beams

No more bear witness of the deathless day,
In the far spaces of the boundless world,
Beyond the circuit of the earth's proud eye
And yet so impotent.   Time in its flight
Impetuous all brightness turns to dark
In the dull vision of the world's crude thought,
And sun, and moon, and stars, in the dim sight
Of man's discernment in the pale of sense,
Decline, and grope, and in the deep submerge
Of doom and death, and nature's dark despair.
Yet he who, gifted with a nobler heart
And truer evidence of worth within,
Foresees the low horizon of his west,
As down his sunset slope he swiftly glides,
Courts his composure, and his wasting hours
Still yields to service of kin, kith, and kind,
The while anticipant of the last step
That enters the abyss, his purpose grand.
Thus Passaconnaway, the sachem high,
Beheld the sun of his exalted day
In haste declining to the western eve,
To set forever to the world that waits
But on appearance and illusion, vain,
Yet e'er potential, in time's stubborn thought,
To foster doubt, and dread, and dismal doom.
Yet he, the wise Bashaba, with his face
Turned to the night's dim curtain, soon to drop

Across his life's late pathway, in full calm
And confidence of soul, his purpose gave
Still to his people and their profit vast.
In fair example in the end that proves
Man's true advantage in the sphere of time,
The pledge and promise sure to high and low,
He spurned rude, wild concerns, and in his thought
Ignored all aims that on aspiring worth
Impose but sorrow and relentless woe.

One day, one solemn day, of counsel wise,
Of wishes eminent for lasting good
And happiness, prolonged in time's awards
For his own people, Passaconnaway,
The chief of chiefs, and mighty in emprise
Of hopeful virtue to his tribes that leaned
Upon his wisdom, in convention large,
At oft Pentucket, met his chiefs and braves,   '
And opened all his heart in words that thrilled
Deep in their bosoms; for he spoke as one
Who last monition of earth's folly takes
And, to the ears that list again no more
His faithful word, transfers in tones of awe
His warning. "Brothers, chiefs, and braves," he said,
" In silence hear my speech, for I am old,
And, like the sapless tree that casts its leaves,
And in the autumn blast sways to its fall,

I totter to the end that lays me low
On earth's cold bosom.   Ere the winds pass by
And leave me lifeless on the damp, chill ground,
I leave you this, my counsel.   Ye have known
How, ere the paleface came to spy the land,
We held him foe and strove in vain to find
The means of his prevention; and, your chief
And greater sachem, man of medicine,
More famed than any other in the tribes
That roam this region, I against him wrought
My swift enchantments unto fruitless ends
And wasted strength: [45] and now he thrives to fill
The world where once he strayed a lonely child
And feeble stranger.   Yet, for judgment lacked
In our first thought, we now have wisdom lent
For right direction in the path that leads
Where dwells our safety.   Mark the words I speak!
Bashaba, I have light than of the sun,
And of the moon, and of the silent stars,
More eminent.   Within my spirit dwells
The wisdom of the Manit, and he bids
Me chide your folly that would oft inspire
The deeds of dire destruction that return
To blast the hearts that hasten to the heat
Of rude, rash rage that seeks with zest to spoil
The plan of the Great Spirit, who with might
Resistless e'er fulfills his wish and work

Through all the tumults of his children, fierce
In their mad fury.   In the paleface tribe,
The Sachem of the world has shown us worth
That claims our profit; for the day has dawned
That seeks our greater comfort of the wealth
That, like sweet water from the mountain side,
From nobler life and action springs to cheer
The spirit thirsting for some purer zeal
And truer purpose.   By this truth ye oft
Have my example tested.   Ye have seen
My purpose in the law that turns our feet
From savage paths and leads us to the place
Of fairer pleasure; and ye know that erst
I of the wise, good powwow sought a heart
To come among us and his counsel give,
To save our lives and peace until the day
When the Great Spirit of the world at last
Shall of each thought take notice, and no brave
Shall e'er be able from his eye to hide
In the thick darkness.   Now, my chiefs and braves,
My brothers all, in my last counsel, hear
The message of the Manit.   Strive ye not
Against the English.   From the sunrise land,
Across the wide, deep water, come the braves
With hearts of stone, and faces red with wrath,
And weapons swift for blood, to crush the land
That tempts the Manit's anger, when he lends

His fury to displeasure.   See the storm
That from the sunset sky breaks from the heat,
With mighty wind, and thunder long and loud,
And lightning swift and sharp, and dashes down
The tall trees of the wood, and all the field
Lays waste with wild confusion of the strength
Of stern destruction!   So will ye your peace
And pride find desolate who seek to stay
The arm of the Great Spirit.   I have done.
My sun goes down.   My brightness seeks the shade.
The deep, dark west drowns all the daylight dim."

INTERLUDE.

IN silent night, a slumber, deep,
　Lethean, chains the world; on high
　The wakeful stars dumb vigils keep;
　　Earth's breast is faint to breathe a sigh.

In sovran night, stern darkness bears
　The scepter; then, with trembling flame,
Each watchfire burns; time's aspect wears
　A veil of awe, subdued and tame.

In solemn night, beneath the dome,
　For dread concern, we fall and pray,—
" Sweet love-lights, guide our spirits home,
　Through crystal depths, to realms of day!"

THE great Bashaba, man of many days,[46]
   Of chiefs the pride and glory of his braves,
In quiet sought the solace of his age,
And, in the comfort of the forest, field,
And flowing fountain of the endless hills,
Life's sunset watched till all the placid west
Beamed with bright beauty in the mellow scene
Of night approaching in the twilight fair;
Yet, of conception just of useful ends
In time established, he example still
Of fair advantage furnished to his brave
Of prestige emulous.   For civil rights,
In bounds determined by the law that makes
All social good established, firm and just,
He made petition, being subject true
And loyal of the state that English rule
Made possible, for peace and plenty framed.
Then the glad paleface chief, in zeal discreet,
In presence of such judgment, free, and fraught
With deep consideration, purpose rare,
And prospect great, of welfare to the tribes
Auspicious, lent his royal hand and seal
To the right project, and Bashaba gave,
Within the fertile vale of Merrimack,
Of land a spacious tract—to east and west
Three miles, and three to north and south—the stream
The whole dividing, half on either side,

While, in the bosom of the river bright,
Lay two green islands, jewels rich and rare.[47]
Here Passaconnaway, once savage chief,
But now a civil sachem, found his rest
And ransom permanent, his manhood crowned.
Within his wigwam rude, but still of home,
In civil order fixed and aspect kind,
The just expression, oft his tribal kin
He gave swift welcome, and his wisdom made
The profit of his sons, and sons of sons,[48]
And of his braves, that oft an insight craved
Of the great future, unto prudent ends
And faithful aims devoted; and betimes,
When some deep fervor of his spirit rose
To heights above earth's privilege but found
Of subjects mortal, he monition urged
And counsel gave of hints, and hopes, and helps
That trend on things immortal, while his thought
E'er fostered some great faith of instinct true
And comprehension vast of life, and love,
And lore unsearchable to sense that gropes
But in the shadow of earth's fancy vain
And time's forlorn despair,—though all his mind
Was shrouded in the gloom that nature sheds
In the crude soul barbaric. Then the last,
Soft, smiling rays of sunset lingered low
In the dim, far horizon, and he lay

Upon his couch of furs, and in his thought
Still dwelt on worth that, wrought within,
E'er lives, and thrives, and triumphs in the face
Of death and dissolution ; while with zeal,
Serene but firm, on lips that feebly broke
The accents of his being, straight he bore
The test of his exemption from time's care
And terror's dark delusion.   As he sank
Fast to the curtained dark of twilight's close,
Once o'er his features wan a strange concern
Crept like a passing shade.   In whispered tones,
But earnest accents, great Bashaba said,
" What means this tumult ? "   Then attendants kind
With haste replied, "A man of medicine
Would ease your heart." [49]   Then he, Bashaba wise,
From soulful depths responded, " Of his skill
I need no comfort, since the Name I own
Which is all medicine."   A thoughtful brave
Then explanation asked, and of the Name
Mysterious craved knowledge ; for he would
Die grandly when the nightly shadows fell
Across the pathway of earth's daytime late.
Then Passaconnaway, the sachem true,
Breathed his last message to the world that wore
The woe of his departure.   " In his breast
Who hears the Manit's voice," he softly said,
"And heeds his counsel, Wisdom works to mould

His being unto newness in the form
Of the Great Spirit's Son, a Chief in life,
And Sachem strong in death, and, like the sun,
His own bright splendor, for his name is Light,
And Light he is, and in his Light he lives
To know no darkness.   In this Light I walk
Straight to the shadow which no shadow is
Before the dawning in the endless day.
Farewell!   I go!   The morn is in the east!
The stars go out!   The moon fades in the west!
The mighty Sun commands the boundless sky!"

POSTLUDE.

BRIGHT Messenger of holy love,
    Whose thought surveys this earthly scene,
  In mercy stooping like a dove
      Through paths of atmosphere serene,
  Our wisdom in obscure lines
      Perceives thy sacred, vast designs.

This world is but a tiny space,
    Of avenues and measures less
Than thy least gift requires to trace
    Its fullest art to lure and bless;
The bounties of thy free discharge
    Demand God's whole creation large.

We catch but glimpses of thy smile
    And whispers of thy cheerful voice
Who yet shall own thy face, the while
    We mingle in thy counsels choice,
Fruition crowning hope, as we
    Shall gain thy ampler courts and thee.

THE LAST POWWOW.

PRELUDE.

———

THE heart doth yearn for purer zeal intense,
   But when devotion swift doth often pour
Earth's fullest cup, it weeps for love's expense
     That is no more.

The fruitful mind doth delve for treasure rich,
   Yet longs for riches, for the world's emprise
Yields not the gem of gems, truth's jewel which
     Still deeper lies.

In present fields, life's patient hands the wheat
   Of harvest reap, but when the constant sun
Sinks to the west, their rest is incomplete,
     Their work undone.

So hope doth dream, and ever dreaming gains
   Its fondest pledge, that he who zest instills
In the quick soul, where larger room obtains,
     Its ends fulfills.

THE LAST POWWOW.

THE thoughtful mind that dwells on problems deep,
    And scans life's broad arena, where the hopes,
The cares, the struggles, of men's hearts, involved
In virtue's mazes or the chains of vice,
Of strange causation contemplation oft
Indulges; and, though scenes of lustrous pride
Of nature's beauty tempt reflection light,
The law's great theme of destiny profound
Still oft compels the soul to aspects grave,
And stirs impressions mighty in the man
Who ponders on the aims that peace impart
And safety promise in the sphere of time.

Across the fertile vale of Merrimack,
Where nestles by the stream the city fair,
New Hampshire's regal seat,[1] one looks and sees,
With freshness, verdure, and with bloom bedight,
The invitation lavish unto dreams,
Illusive, sweet; but then, perchance, he turns,
In fancy's wandering through varied fields,
And touches on the border-land of hints

5

That into distance stray, to grasp the wish
And worth that, in the restless, throbbing breasts
Of ancient sachems [2] of the valley rich,
Forecast in smiles or frowns eventful fate:
And thus his muse grows solemn till he dwells
Alone on hopes that were, and yet were not,
In Wisdom's stern decree, time's test to try.

It may have been, one day, one distant day,
That old Pehaungun in his wigwam sat,
Last of the Penacooks,[3] and, in sad thought,
Beheld the shining river and its vale
Of smiling beauty; and, in musing long
On strength and pride departed of the tribe—
His sires and brothers—that the land once claimed
In prestige undisputed, with his face
All dark with doubt and heaviness of heart,
He haply craved within his heaving breast
Some meed of cause in explanation found
Of such despair and devastation wrought
Upon his people, peerless, proud, but pressed
To painful proneness of their prestige prompt,
Their star just setting in the silver sheen
Of the dim twilight.   Here we skill invoke
To tell a tale—as if Pehaungun lent
An eager ear—and reason ripe disclose
And profit pledge to him who hears and heeds.

INTERLUDE.

THE rose, unfolding in a smile,
 When day has just begun,
Yet grieves, her brightness less the while
 Than luster in the sun;

And when a lark, full glad to greet
 The morning, springs on high,
He saddens that his flight, so fleet,
 Is still below the sky;

And I, in joy each early day,
 Muse with afflatus strong,
Yet mourn that skill cannot portray
 My love, the queen of song.

THE dim, old days of ancient life and lore,
 Within the valley ever bright and fair,
Evolve, in contemplation of the soul,
The story of great fame and wondrous pride
In puissance of honor. Ere the march
Of civil progress, by the English wrought,
Usurped the wide domain of waste and wild
In high New Hampshire, here indeed was known
Such wisdom in command of men and moods
As ever admiration stirs in those
Who mark great triumphs and approval give

To thoughtful excellence in rightful rule.
The sachem wise, chief Passaconnaway,[4]
Of Penacooks the potentate supreme
By law's inheritance, had roused the tribe
To valor high and prestige far renowned.
Of instincts prescient, of aims and ends
Constructive in the sphere of royal sway,
Of lofty motive urged, and grander scheme
Made manifest, this savage sachem, rude,
But still magnificent in noble mind,
And mien, and purpose, many tribes had led
To wise confederation, and they held
Their rights and wishes common, save that he,
Bashaba[5] named, great Passaconnaway,
Child of the Bear,[6] was sovran lord of all,
While Penacook was found, the pristine tribe,
Of honor first, in name and fame elate.

Thus ruled Bashaba, mighty prince and head
Of tribes that told not less than four times four
In thriving numbers, daring chiefs and braves,
Each sannup with his squaw and children oft,
A savage multitude that raged and roamed
Far by the ocean strand and inland surged,[7]
A host then countless,—and its strength was firm.
Nor was such aspect prosperous the prize
Alone of prowess in the field of war

And fearless conquest; for, Bashaba, wise
In ripe discernment of time's issues vast,
Had counseled prudence in the sphere of thought
And act administrative, peace esteemed
And safety pleaded, with life's worth that trends
On things supernal held in choice emprise
Of potent strict assertion.   He had said,—
" Be wise before the Manit, he who lives,
Chief of our lives and days, and in the hearts
Of his true braves works wisdom unto wish
And worth beneficent; and he in me,
His spirit prompting mine, has made me clear
To see your hope triumphant, or your fear
In doom destructive, as you list my word
Or close your ear and hold my counsel naught."[8]

Time's scenes have oft transition, and our days
Oft wend to change that e'er of heart and mind
Takes wiser counsel, and who haply lays
His grasp on larger knowledge, for his guide
Upon the path progressive, gains the prize
Of noble emulation, and his soul
Confirms in hope and prospect in the van
Of life that prospers unto virtue's goal.
The savage realm by Passaconnaway
Held subject, in the sway of rarer zeal
And richer zest of honor, in full test

Had privilege of profit, when the sun
Of civil splendor in the social east
Rose on its night, to light its gloom afar,
And wake response in actions of the day,
Born of the scheme redemptive of the souls
That plodded but in ways of darkness wild.
The English came, with art and science, bent
On greater demonstration of the worth
In social life potential, and—to crown
The weal in time's ends possible—the faith
And pledge of life eternal, in the sphere
Of righteous merit, manifest to souls
That longed for peace perpetual, when thought
Revolved the world's vain promise.   In the van
Of the crude prospects of the savage mind,
Such advent grew portentous in the dread
Of sudden devastation in the ways
And walks accustomed ; and, with swift emprise,
Great fear all hearts assailed, and savage braves,
To nameless prowess trained, in trembling mien
The future held in contemplation grave.
In such presentment of the time that tried
The soul barbaric, Passaconnaway,
Bashaba, chief of chiefs, and mighty man
In counsel sage, but greater still in gifts
That ends foresee beyond the shady bounds
Of time and sense, but feeble in the sphere

Of truth's discernment, in his spirit rose
Above the mists of doubt and, with the eye
Of judgment prescient of grander aims
Within the Manit's purpose, gave his heart
To the great prospect, and his subjects urged
To thoughts and acts prudential in the sphere
Of wisdom provident of sense and soul.
In faithful zeal, within the concourse great
Of chiefs and braves, he made his urgent plea,
And bore his attestation straight and strong,
And said, " My chiefs and brothers, braves and friends,
Give ear and hear my speech, for I am he
Whose spirit talks with Manit, and I know
The thing to come and see the prospect far
Of your true safety.   In the English cause
Lies your hereafter.   With the paleface strive
No more in future.   In his will, and work,
And worship shall the redskin tribes obtain
Their promise certain.   Lo ! The Manit rides
Upon the wind that fells the stoutest tree,
And on the wave that sweeps the ocean shore
And leaves naught that resists it.   In the law
And service of the time that dawns anew,
Like sunshine in the east, let us behold
Our patient peace and plenty till we come,
Well and with joy, where rests the soul of care
In life's true wigwam.   With this counsel firm,

Take my example.   From the wild I turn
To seek the fruit that from the fertile field
I pluck with pleasure in the plan that proves
The worth of wisdom.   Thus shall all my days
See sunshine soft and sweet, till in the west
The daylight dies in darkness deep of death,
Yet cast in calm, a sighless summer eve." [9]
Thus great Bashaba spoke, and kept his word,
And to the civil law of English mode,
Adherence gave, and on his own estate,
By line and scroll determined, kept his peace
And nourished profit, till life's end the type
Of manhood mild and meek, of virtue vast.

INTERLUDE.

THOU, of royal gifts, to me
   Earth's tokens, time's endowments choice,
I gladden for thy grace, by thee
   In beauty's excellence rejoice,
Yet once I tune a cheerful lay
For that which will not pass away.

How subtly the presentment came,
   When first we met, as I beheld,
With longing gaze, thy tender flame
   Of rising beams, that doubt dispelled,
As hope descried each trembling ray
And prayed it might not pass away.

Now is my spirit still; I reap
   The harvest of the boundless charms
That deck thy maidenhood, but keep
   My soul intent on thine, which arms
My steadfast heart, that dreams for aye
Love lasts and cannot pass away.

BETIMES a noble soul, in virtue's path,
   The standard of the truth in high emprise
Holds up before the world, and, full of zeal
For profit excellent and prospect wise,
In thought impulsive, deems the triumph swift
Of priceless rectitude, at once, at hand,
And feasts his soul observant on the wealth
Expectant in the promise of his dream,
Cast in the realm ideal.   This, a world,
Of instinct sensuous, of passion wild,
Of vain reflection selfish—in the moods
Of mindless method in the sphere of dread
Of true or false designs on pleasure dear
Or privilege exemptive—slowly grasps
The fact conservative of right and rule
In Wisdom's work prudential.   He who looks
Beyond the present to the future day,
Of ripe fruition of some grander scheme
Of judgment popular, has sorest need
Of patience puissant, endurant, long,

In his heart's travail for the worth he waits.
Great Passaconnaway, the sachem rare,
This theme attested in his own true soul
And mind, anticipant of nobler aims
And ends more eminent, within the bound
Of the great circle social.   His was hope
That slight reward found certain, and his sun
Went down the west, to shed its last, pale beams
Upon a world still wasting wealth of will
In wildest worthlessness.   A purpose vile,
In social friend or foe, in savage clan
Or civil conclave, oft, in strife for gain
And haste unhallowed, passion fierce enraged
And fell destruction prompted ; and as e'er
In contests dire of simple forces weak
With energies compounded, staunch, and strong,
The ranks of redmen shrank before the rush
And rant of palefaced anger, skilled to bear
The ardor more disastrous.   Thus was fate
Made unpropitious to the tribe that bore
The name of Penacook, choice treasure found
Of zeal in the Bashaba : yet the mind
And instinct barbarous, in rash design
For privilege delusive, set the snare
Of liberty's own doom, and life's despair,
And death's grim exultation in the face
Of virtue horrified, the fiend of vice

Exalted without mercy.   From the east,
By civil transportation, came a foe,
Dread occuwee,[10] the liquid hot that burned
The soul's own wigwam, while death's demons danced
Within the lurid light, and howled in glee
Of frantic furor, till damnation's glare
And dizzy whirling drew all subjects in
And down to one deep vortex, hopeless, huge.
Such things Bashaba saw and inly grieved.

The cause and course that consummation seek
On the sad road to ruin fail not oft
Of counsel provident of worth exposed
And weal endangered.   In the highway rash
Oft stands a monitor, of aspect firm,
And word emphatic, but with zest that bears
The burden of the bane that follows fast
Upon the track of each whom folly leads
To the sure goal destructive.   Thus a chief,
Tahanto,[11] wise and prudent, while the blood
Of tribal royalty within his veins
Coursed freely, strove in vain with zeal to stay
The march infernal, moved by occuwee,
And cried, " Pour out !   Pour out !   The ground may
    take
The drink that makes us devils, all as one
Bent on bad deeds of doom to friend or foe ! "[12]

Nor did example swift in projects wise,
Borne by the chief of chiefs, full oft to praise
Inviting choice expression, lack its meed
Of faithful emulation, when the tide
Of dark events surged downward.   There was one,
A chief indeed, brave Wonalancet, son
Of Passaconnaway, an offspring true
Of the great, good Bashaba, and he gave
His heart to wisdom and his soul to peace,
And sure salvation of his people sought,
Himself in regal power.   Once he heard
The great apostle to the redmen sent—
The pious Eliot—and felt the flow
Of ferventness divine within his breast
Move, melt, and mould his spirit in the form
Of the Almighty Son, who lives, and loves,
And in the end makes happy all the man,
In gentle mien recast, and yet of skill
To prosper unto virtue more and more
In the true life eternal.[13]   Then great war,
With furor fierce for blood, and dark with death,
The whole land menaced, while full oft its strokes
Laid low the innocent, or near, or far,
The thrifty home made desolate, the tribes,
Urged by great Philip, seeking endless woe
In full destruction for the paleface bands
Wherever clustered :[14] and the son and chief,

True Wonalancet, freed from vengeance quick,
And prescient of prudence, like his sire,
His warriors swift withdrew from tempting haunts,
And, in recesses deeper of the wild,
Where mountains reared their heads in silent thought,
And babbling streams in peaceful accents talked,
And lisping leaves in tones of pity sighed,
He watched the war-clouds distant, ere the storm
Broke clear, and sunshine cast its cheerful rays
Far on the landscape of a thankful world,
From the dark tempest rescued.   Then he came
Forth from the wilderness, in mercy's strength
To render deeds of gladness to the heart
That hung on horror's fate, while yet the land
Beheld some burden of the strife that e'er
From time to time clashed foes and victims found,
Or civil, or barbaric.[15]   English law
Held sway at fair Cocheco.[16]   Thither went
Wise Wonalancet and submission made
To civil order, and to judgment, wrought
Of wider prescience of use and weal,
Looked for redemption of his time and tribe.
His purpose true his act gave sure attest,
And when, with rash conceit of vengeance vain,
A band of thoughtless braves a mother kind
And five fair children—widow clad in weeds
And offspring piteous—of English blood,

Held in fierce bondage and to death consigned,
The angry flames to feed on guileless flesh
Already burning, Wonalancet came
With glad salvation, and their safety made
Both sure and sudden, and to civil heart
And savage sense made worth and wisdom clear.[17]
Yet madness ruled the tribe, and hopes and aims
Redemptive in the few had weak emprise.

INTERLUDE.

WE leave thee with the silent past,
   Responsive to no present call;
Thy rarest pleasures could not last,
   Thy gifts are shrouded with a pall:
     O sere old days,
     O sad old days,
  Thy spring became untimely fall!

Within thy trusted hands were laid
   The pledges of our cares discreet;
The sacred debt ye never paid,
   Thine was a staff, nor sure, nor feat:
     O weak old days,
     O wan old days,
  Thy chaff disclosed no promised wheat!

Proud hopes, resplendent as elate,
  Were of thy sweet assurance born;
Ye read no true decrees of fate
  And broke our tender hearts forlorn:
    O dull old days,
    O dead old days,
  Thine is the night that knows no morn!

THE world is witness oft of sudden change
  In things administrative, as when one
To some one other yields the regal palm
And scepter, and preëminence resigns,
In sequence unavoidable in life
And lot uncertain. In the march of time,
The royal tribe of Penacook oft found
A sachem subsequent to sachem proud,
And saw in sway transition—hapless when
The worse for better rule, in days that merged .
On degradation, sped still faster on
The fell events that crown a dark despair
Of ends and aims of aspiration high.
Wise Wonalancet in his turn gave o'er
The chieftain's precedence,[18] and fortune ill
Bore witness of disaster in the moods
Of him succeeding. Kancamaugus, vain
In base ambition, on delusion bent
In vile conspiracy, the tribe drew on

In the wild path of folly till its course
Far to the dismal west of deadly doom
In woe proceeded.[19]   In Cocheco town,
In false security, the aged chief
Of English arms, gray Waldron, in his hold
Of fancied strength, resided, and reposed,
And justice executed, yet withal
He bore the mien complacent when a brave
Or squaw sought shelter of his kindly roof
Within his fortress, of the day or night
A wearied guest with welcome unto rest
And rich refreshment to the savage soul,
To civil comforts stranger.   Thus was he,
The English chief, to apprehension blind,
When earth's last woe beset him, snared, betrayed.[20]
A summer eve grew dim, and two mild squaws
Besought his shelter, and he gave them cheer
And favor generous ; and as the hour
Sped to the night full dark, the guests, in thought
Of their great host's conception of his peace
And safe precaution, spoke and lightly said,—
" What if the Indians, the braves estranged,[21]
Should come to-night ? "   Then he, with zeal intense
And flushing cheek, declared,—"A hundred men
As brave as breathe the air would hear my word,
And spring with vengeance on the reckless foe,
And smite him without mercy, till he fell

In the deep, bloody pit his madness made
For his own danger deadly!"[22]   Then the night
Its darkest curtain drew, and all was still,
Yet so with dire foreboding.   In the dark,
The faithless squaws, in league with braves alert
For sharp revenge for wrongs, or true, or false,[23]
Arose and stealthily the door unbarred
And gave the foe admission.   Old and gray,
The English chieftain, roused from sleep profound,
Of swift defence took counsel, and his sword
He wielded in defiance till he drove
The wild assailants close upon the door
Of their departure from the fortress strong;
He then recoiling for an arm more sure
In death's quick dealing, forth upon him sprung
The savage victors, who their angry taunt—
" Who now shall judge the Indians? "[24]—enforced
With fierce resentment till his streaming blood
Paid forfeit of their fury.   Rudely bound
And helpless in his chair, the hoary chief
The cruel fiends upon a table placed
In mocking state, and, passing one by one,
Each brave his knife drew twice across his flesh
And said, " Thus my accounts I now cross out! "
Till, with infernal mutilation scarred,
The paleface warrior, bleeding, drooped, and died,
His spirit fleeing from the clay inthralled
6

In dreadful, dumb despair.   With rage beset
On fell destruction far, the restless braves
Their bloody vengeance plied till all the town,
In horror of distress, its witness bore
To the great tragedy, as matrons, maids,
And men of sterner mould, with children clad
In mourning mien too somber for their age,
Wept for their losses, and their hearts consigned
To grief too deep for words, and in the walks
Of sorrow bowed in heaviness, their tears
In silence coursing down their pallid cheeks.[25]
Such madness, conversant of rash designs
In wildest execution, on the tribe
That in its purpose mingled cast a gloom
Rebuking and suspicious, and its ranks,
Once full and fair, in doubt, and dread, and doom,
Fast shrank away, to far dispersion urged
Among the savage circles of the north,[26]
The fame of Penacook, once bright, now merged
In creeping shades oblivious of night.

INTERLUDE.

THE morn is fair in the sunlight's glare!
Swift pleasures glide as the swallows fly,
And a heart says once, through a face most rare,
Good-day and then good-bye.

O the day is bright in the noontide's height!
  Sweet blossoms smile though the breezes sigh,
And a heart is sad, in the sparkling light
    Good-day, for dull good-bye.

O the daylight glows at the evening's close!
  Rich hues exult if the leaves but die,
And a heart is glad for the end that knows
    Good-day but not good-bye.

THE aspects of our moral life are cast
  In moods reciprocative, though its strength
May lapse to weakness.   On the shores of time,
The ocean waves break high and then return,
To break again with ardor, though the tide
Still ebbs with force far to the deep abyss
Of the dark waters.   Though the name, and fame,
And puissance of Penacook swept fast
To the dim distance of the thoughts of men
In themes historic skillful, yet was worth
Not in one surge of fortune's ebbing tide
Engulfed, to sight extinguished.   In the days
That saw the slow decline, full oft some zeal
Of nobler instinct in the redman's soul
This truth attested.   White men [27] once—a scout—
On future weal intent, the land to spy,
Came to the township new, which English law

Had fixed at Penacook [28] for settlers true,
To civil ends devoted, and they craved
A sojourn for the winter in the place
Where yet should be plantations, full of life,
And thrift, and fair prosperity, the arts
Of peace triumphant in the patient toil
Of manhood virtuous, and wise, and kind.
The strangers lingered, but when wintry storms
And tempests unpropitious had their hearts
Discomfited with want and sadness wan,
They drooped in peril of their case forlorn,
Death on them staring.   Then the redmen—few
And scattered fragments of the once great tribe
Of royal Penacooks—their spirits moved
To pity for sad lack, the white men gave
A portion of their plenty and made glad
The soul of sore privation.   Thus a touch
Of friendship, that the whole world's kinship proves,
In degradation deep expressed the good
That lives when fate with face averted frowns.

True virtue wins approval, though its spark
Burns feebly in the soul, when conscience, weak,
In limping aspect falters, and the man
Upon life's highway gropes in moral moods
That e'er forebode the consummation dark
Of bright worth's obscuration.   In the day

Of civil culture, dawning on the wild
Of ancient Penacook, there flamed the zeal—
In faithful ardor of the heart, enshrined
In holy impulse, of ambition sped
By purpose consecrated, and to acts
Of humbleness devoted unto peace
That the world's pleasure passes—patiently
To win the soul barbaric, and the faint,
Slight worth invite to wisdom.   In the band
Of English settlers came the priest of God—
The pious Walker [29]—and his love benign
Warmed to the Indian whose heart might burn
With love's returning fire of Goodness caught
And grace renewed in never ending glow.
The holy man the pious thought instilled,
And roused intention godly, and the mind
To wisdom's uses pointed, while his faith
He fain attested by his works sincere,
To admonition equal; and he gave
Oft pledges of his word, and to the tribe,
In strength declining, showed fraternal mood
And kindly mien, and to his hearth bespoke
The social welcome, while his presence oft
The wigwam cheered with sweet and sacred light
That beamed like soft effulgence of the rays
That break from Heaven's sun on summits high
Of God's eternal mountains, when the clouds,

With slight disparting, let the brightness through.
Yet condescension more his purpose proved
Of confidential fervor, as his son,
A stripling young and tender,[30] oft he lent
To light the redman's camp with luster choice
Of innocence and joy, to be in pride
Of childish fancy decked with feathers rare,
And thus returned, a paleface sachem, small
But filled with gladness of the spirit cast
In childhood rapt, great glory's guise assumed.

A soul may stem though it may never stay
The tide that surges to the sure extreme
Of life's wild waves reactive.   Though the priest,
In pious prudence, unto virtue urged
The Penacooks, declining in their might
And manhood, still the tide that, swelling, bore
Upon its height no destiny sublime
Within the grasp of mortals, swept its prey
On to extinction in the goal of time,
To leave no trail, or trace, or track behind.
The redman's pride departed till the chief,
Ignoble sachem, for base occuwee,
The bad fire-water, e'en his rights conveyed
To the shrewd paleface, who his gain invoked
In his weak rival's passion.   Thus the grace
Of sachems proud, from great Bashaba wise

To Wattanummon[31] foolish, waned and fled
In fateful degradation.   Sad truth tells
The doleful tale.   One shining, summer day,
Stout Ebenezer Eastman,[32] with his scythe,
Would fain a meadow[33] mow; and when his skill
The thrifty verdure laid in swiftness low,
The chief depraved came forth, and swung his arms,
And cried, " My grass! My grass! No cut! No cut!"
But when calm Eastman poured in keen design
And gave the sachem drink to soothe his blame,
The chief's resentment softened with the flow
Of light, good nature, in his spirit stirred
By occuwee, till once again he spoke
With voice emphatic, spreading forth his hands,
And said, "Your grass! Your grass! You cut! You
        cut !"
Thus Eastman purchased freely, day by day,
The field's wild bounty and his wealth increased.

Yet honor saw a deeper shade of gloom.
The instinct virtuous, that each to each
Makes pure and peaceful in the sacred walks
Of love domestic, falters not, nor fails,
In the true soul of man.   The subtle snare,
The unseen blow, the theft of treasure choice
Of the fond heart's devotion, spring not forth
Save from the spirit craven in the zeal

Of passion devilish of reason damned.
Not oft indeed in savage life has lust
Such vile fruition.　Yet what mind forecasts
What depth depraved some sinking soul may find,
The social frame corrupted?　Let this tale
In brief rehearse the story.　In a day,
A luckless shadow gloomed across the path
Of a crude sachem[84] of the hapless tribe
Whose sorrows prompt recital.　To his home,
In a fell hour unguarded, came the foe—
A brave degraded—and his squaw induced
To faithless flight unholy.　Up the stream—
The pleasant Merrimack—the culprits took
Their stealthy way till, on a verdant isle,[85]
They sought the shelter of the sinful night,
Awaiting morn's still farther transit, found
Of daring fault upon the friendly way
Of the deep wild to north.　The sachem wronged,
Yet vengeful, swiftly up the stream pursued
The guilty pair, and near their foul retreat
Their soon emergence watched ; and when they took
Again their swift canoe, full well to speed
Their flight still onward, then his gun's good aim
Their double death decided.　In the waves,
Their breathless forms sank deep till vision lost
Each dank, doomed trace sepulchral, till one day,
Lodged halfway home, in ghastly plight and pale,

Upon the verdant bank the dead squaw lay,
Where designation still narration oft
Revives in fame unhallowed, shameful, sad.[36]

INTERLUDE.

WHERE is a morn more east than east:
  The thrill of bright, pure love that springs
  Out of the dawn of gladsome things,
  So like a bird on buoyant wings,
Floats on the morn more east than east.

There is a glow more south than south:
  The ardor of the thankful heart
  That bears in virtue's sphere its part,
  Evolved like bloom in lustrous art,
Flames from the glow more south than south.

There is a chill more north than north:
  The dismal shiver in the blast
  Of conscience o'er a barren past,
  As shrinks the startled fawn, aghast,
Is of the chill more north than north.

There is a night more west than west:
  The flight that grovels in the dark
  Of life bereft of honor's spark,
  The foe's despair, unsheltered, stark,
Gropes to the night more west than west.

THE sad narration falters to its close,
   And little lore now lingers to express
The low descending climax of the tale
That ends in wretchedness of will and work
In the lost tribe degraded.   Yet as turns
The story to the verge and solemn bound
Of its relation dolorous, what change,
In sudden mood, affects and blanches pale
The face of brave Pehaungun, listing long
The slow recital?   Old,[37] and weak, and wan,
He bears the burden of the woes that fill
His tribe's regretful history, and feels
The feeble props of life declining yield
Beneath their load too weighty.   In the pain,
That wounds his heart, and in his shrouded mind
Throbs unto misery intense and deep,
His spirit seeks transition, and its flight
To the unseen hereafter claims at length
In silent resignation, doleful, dumb.
His eyelids droop, his breath fails, short and faint,
His form sways helplessly, and at the last
The earth's cold bosom takes his prostrate length,
In aspect lifeless. [38]   To his wigwam come
The scattered remnants of his clan, to raise
The dismal wail, and rites sepulchral give
Their dead companion, brother, friend, and brave,
Of their own blood partaker.   Of a tree—

The forest pine full large—a section long
Becomes a rude, rough coffin, to the core
By fire persistent hollowed—or the space
The blunt, stone chisel renders free to hold
The soulless form within—while, for a lid,
The bark proves full enclosure.   Then a grave,
Deep in the ground by excavation made,
Receives the tribute of death's dismal doom.
The savage sannups, mindless of the scenes
That calm solemnity of nobler souls
Claim ever in the sphere of virtue tried
By fate resistless, lend their hearts profane
To madness weird and wild, and to the sky
Send up loud cries infernal, as they tramp
The damp earth down upon the dead man's breast,
And shout aloud, " He no get out ! " till oft
" He no get out ! " the welkin far resounds.
Nor does distraction base in deathstruck minds
Cease its wild tumult when, by earth enclosed,
The helpless form assumes its endless rest
In the dread pit eternal.   Still they keep
Their fierce carousal, and when day to night
Turns black with shadows, all the darkness deep
Strange horror haunts with hellish howling, heard
In the far distance, till strong occuwee
The reckless riot turns to deathlike sleep
Upon the senseless ground ; and all are still
Till outraged nature wakes in shame full sore.

INTERLUDE.

WITHIN my quiet chamber, where
   Composure kind enchantment brings,
For restless grief, I oft repair
   And listen to a hope that sings.

There life's pulsation softly beats,
   As subject to a strict command,
And calmly thought in guise entreats
   A message from a far-off land.

Then, while the zephyr lightly plays
   To voices of the distant years,
A promise hymns of coming days
   And melts my passive soul that hears.

Swift moments flee; I rise and go,
   With pearly drops my eyelids hung,
Nor cause divine; I only know
   My heart is full; sweet hope has sung.

THOUGH old and sad Pehaungun lists no more
   The rueful tale of prestige lost and gone,
In fancy's light conceit, the thought of time,
In witness of the dim events of eld,
When Penacooks, in degradation low,
Held scarce a foothold of their ancient realm,

Turns to the fitful, fateful, closing scene
Of the stern tragedy this volume bears
To future kind remembrance of the years.
In the vast scheme composite of the world,
And earthly incidents in time involved,
Some co-relation e'er all facts attest,
Appendent to, dependent on, and bound
By law each to each other.   In the course
Of life that far ascends in social ways,
Or equally descends in paths convened
Of things associated, good with good,
Or ill with ill, is manifested e'er
In each department common.   Thus to live,
Or die, together, all our gifts, and moods,
And customs hold involved the end
That each proves worthy, or unworthy shows
Each in itself and fragment of a whole
Corrupted.   This, the truth emphatic, bore
Its own swift witness in the waning day
Of shining honor in the tribe that knew
The great name Penacook in cherished pride.
In such reflections cast, narration bears
In these fast closing lines, description true
Of THE LAST POWWOW, when the remnants few
Of the proud tribe—whose fame in ancient lore
Still fills the land where Penacooks of eld
Found vast prosperity, but still to pine

In poverty disastrous—met once more
For aye in mad convention on the soil
Their great forefathers trod and made the scene
Of wisdom's oft safe counsels.   In the days,
Far distant, when the savage braves upheld
In honor lofty sages—powwows,[39] deep
In knowledge weighty, and of insight keen
In things mysterious to common ken,
And wise to caution or encourage zest
Of deeds impetuous—time's courses ran
To prospects profitable in the sphere
Of life's sublimer action.   Then, for aims
And uses excellent, when braves convened
In moods deliberative, there were found,
In faultless eminence, the powwows, good
And grave, to challenge fate, and give the charge
To prudent ends directing : and when zeal,
In themes exalted, raised their spirits high
In noble ecstacy—till conscience grasped
The truth far reaching, and, in flaming speech
Of eloquence unfeigned, the gifted tongue
Proved all its potency to stem or stay
The flood of hasty passion—to impart
Their fervor to their fellows, then the name,
In swift transfusion with the spirit fired,
From few transferred to many, in the bond
Of fellowship united, thrilled within

The whole assembly, which in fact became
And appellation powwow.   Thus the man
Gives to the mass his title, e'en as Christ,
The name preëminent, in spirit lives
Within all saintly Christians.   Yet will fate
Its strange transitions urge full oft in names,
Nor less full oft in meanings.   In the depth
Of degradation in its foul foray
Upon the plain of passion, soon the tribe
Of Penacook the import sunk in shame
Of powwow, word exalted—name, and act
In full supremacy of noble zeal
In minds concerted unto ends discreet ;
And, counsel turned carousal, then the zest
And ardor of the spirit, in the glow
Of rapt sincerity, no longer roused
Slow manhood virtuous, but, in its stead,
Fierce furor flamed with blasting breath that burned
To the soul's core and scorched with anguish keen
The helpless heart, by occuwee enchained.

The sun of day was hasting to the eve
When fifty braves in name, but yet in state
Impuissant of will that courage takes
In peril of vain passion, concourse held
Upon the banks of Horseshoe,[40] there to lend
Their souls and bodies to the revels foul

Of a great powwow—frenzy hot and fierce
By fateful occuwee, the water charged
With baneful fire of force infernal fed.
With arms and much array of warlike guise,
The riot huge foreseen, with speed they made
Demonic preparation, save that then
An instinct still potential of the man,
Debased and yet susceptible of good,
Stirred in their savage bosoms.   To the east,
A few steps distant, stood the peaceful home
Of wise and pious Walker, he whose heart
Had oft to souls barbaric yearned with love,
Expressed in actions kindly.   All alone,
His fond wife bore the terror of the deeds
Prospective held by savages in vogue
In the long night of horror.   Thoughtful once,
The reckless redskins, counsel taking, said,
"The good man's squaw will break her heart with
          fear
When the loud powwow fills her ear, and she
Shall think upon great danger.   Let us go
Straight to her wigwam strong, and all our bows,
And arrows, knives, and guns, give to her hand
In wise, safe keeping, till the powwow cease,
That she may find her peace and rest till morn:
And when again the good man to his home
Comes smiling in good heart, he then will know

The redman loves his friend and will not hurt
Or make afraid his squaw for wish his own."
Thus to the house the thankful braves, in care,
Of sacred friendship's peril, in the dread
Of fiendish acts uncertain, went, their arms
To the glad matron passing, for her cheer
Of the brief, wild hereafter, in the rouse
Of the impending furor, when their brains,
With occuwee inflamed, hot madness ruled.
Then to the Horseshoe's bank returning, there
They loosed their zeal tempestive in the flow
Of the bad water, save that one, for cause
Protective, kept the skillful watch and ward
Of soberness demanded in the maze
Of mind intoxicated, ruthless, rash.
The shrouded eve beheld the revel dark,
The midnight black observed the horrid din,
The rising morn o'erlooked confusion dumb,
And when the day had stupor waked to sense,
In partial measure potent, to their feet
The fevered braves arose, and, all their arms
In shamefaced mood assuming, turned their gaze
Upon the wilderness with footsteps slow,
The great, Last Powwow [41] ended, for no more
The Penacooks, within the fertile vale
Of Merrimack, mad concourse craved.

7

INTERLUDE.

THE soul, to speak one sacred word,
   More true, pure, blest than all yet heard,
Would leap and carol like a bird.

Hard fate prevents that accent sweet,
By some relation incomplete
Of tongue, or ear, or both to meet.

O life is wedded to a sigh !
The gift divine our lips doth fly
Till time removes, when we shall die.

THE sun revolved to light the patient years ;
   The placid moon, each nightly sequence just,
In motion annual, its mission proved
In soft effulgence ; and the twinkling stars
Serenely from the dome peeped forth and kept
Their dimly faithful watch, when sun and moon
Their faces veiled in shadows, as swift time
Perennial its work alternate held
In strict and true progression.   Yet no more
The once famed Penacooks in solemn mood,
Or mien hilarious, convention found
Within their ancient haunts, to counsel good,
And rouse the spirit earnest for great deeds
Of duty demonstrated, or to stir

The passion purposeless to potent heat
That wrought but doom delusive, worthless, wild.
The scattered remnants of the royal clan—
Once far predominant—their pathways took
To wide dispersion in the wasting ranks
Of tribes fraternal in the blood that ran
In streams congenital from nameless eld.
Then prestige faded dim, and weakly low
Strength waned, and ardor lost its flame
And blazed no more for lofty, proud emprise
Of right and rule contested—fitful zest
Of profit personal, in stealthy deeds
Of cruel desolation, in the sphere
Of service slavish, substituting zeal
In nobler homage of the tribal state,
Or cause confederated, tribe with tribe.
Perchance anon for pelf some dusky scout,
Forth from the nightly dark or forest shade,
An English home assaulted, and weak age
And helpless infancy in death's despair
Laid low and bloody, while the youth and maid,
The man and matron, in a woeful train,
Were hastened to the north, the price to pay
Of zest penurious, when friends, in grief
And dread concern, their loved and lost should gain
By ransom purchased, while the savage fiends
The part but servile played, and to the French,

At war with Englishmen, their lust allied.[42]
But pangs of internecine war no more
The heart domestic rends with bloodstained woe
In fair New Hampshire.   Time was, long ago,
When Englishmen and French their arms resigned
And gave to peace their pleasure.   Kindly aims
And ends industrious the landscape bless
With scenes of present bounty; home, and mart,
And mill, in oft relief of fertile green
Far stretching, prove the worth exalted found
In arts diversified within the vale
Of Merrimack, the river by this theme
And tale conspicuous.   A countless throng
Of souls their stations happy find within
The peaceful valley.—Where indeed are they—
The Indians—the Penacooks once proud—
Who filled this realm of plenty?   From the vast,
On restless, subtle waves the question breathes
To test the heart's compassion.   As the air
Plays softly in the ear, the lisping leaves
Take up its accents, and the forest sighs
Its sweet, sad requiem, and as the breeze
Floats gently down the slopes and stirs the dells,
The swaying ferns and grasses sob and make
Responsive lamentation.   Then still thought,
In tender mood, regretful, hopeful, strong,
The question bears up to the Endless World.

POSTLUDE.

IF aught I have left unsung,
  I will give it to the earth ;
    For the bee knows
    Where the bloom grows,
  And honeyed drops have birth :
  Love's feet have strayed afar,
  Perchance where roses are ;
    The land's delight
    May render bright
My notes from sorrow wrung.

If aught I have left unsung,
  I will give it to the air ;
    For the bird flies,
    When the leaf dies,
  On balmy breezes fair ;
  Sweet love hath flown away,
  Perhaps when zephyrs play—
    Kind winds that make
    Tones glad that break
So sadly on the tongue.

If aught I have left unsung,
  I will give it to the sky ;
    For the stars peep,
    While the shades creep
  But cannot reach so high :
  Love haply finds a rest
  In starry mansions blest,
    While the great dome
    My song takes home,
Where joys from woes have sprung.

NOTES.

NOTES TO THE SEER.

1. Page 7. The Merrimack River, which rises in New Hampshire.

2. Page 7. The name Crystal Hills was given by early explorers of New Hampshire to the White Mountains.

3. Page 10. This imaginary time recedes from the year 1892.

4. Page 10. A spot is conceived on a highland within the limits of the present city of Concord.

5. Page 11. This name is assumed for reasons that appear later. See note 18.

6. Page 11. The native Indians of New Hampshire were of the Algonquin race and of the Nipmuck family.

7. Page 11. The term *Penacook*, the "Crooked Place," refers to the tortuous course of the river Merrimack within the limits of the city of Concord. It appears that the Indians of New Hampshire frequently adopted tribal names from the localities where they resided.

8. Page 11. It is doubtful if the eastern Indians of the present territory of the United States ever employed the

skins of animals in the construction of their wigwams, though there is historic evidence that the western Indians did so. The word noted is used by poetic license.

9. Page 11. An assumed name.

10. Page 11. The Manit, or Manitou, was the supreme deity of the American Indians.

11. Page 12. The Indian sannups, or males of the tribe, only occasionally condescended to labor, work being the special function of the squaws.

12. Page 14. The term *medicine*, as used among the Indians, seems to imply the existence of an occult gift in the man who subjectively adopts it. In astrology, also, people who are born under the special influence of the ascending sun are said to be proud. Some mystics have also asserted that persons who are born under a peculiar aspect of the sun are gifted with a second sight.

13. Page 15. Among the Indians, the rite of burying the tomahawk symbolized the prevalence of peace.

14. Page 16. According to an imperfect tradition, feathers were worn only by chiefs or their sons.

15. Page 17. The Indian idea of making medicine seems to imply something akin to conjuration, while it may mean something like deep introspection, which often absorbs the whole consciousness.

16. Page 18. Deer and wolf was an athletic game played by Indian children.

17. Page 19. The Indian word *powwow* is equivalent to priest or conjurer.

18. Page 22. The name Passaconnaway, from *papoeis*, a child, and *kunnewa*, a bear, seems by right of analogy to demand the penultimate consonant we give it. The interpretation "Child of the Bear" suggests the assumed name of Kunnewa, ascribed to Passaconnaway's father.

19. Page 23. An assumed name.

20. Page 23. See Whittier's poem, "The Bridal of Penacook," for an account of "Weetamoo," or Wanuchus, who married "Winnipurkit," chief of the tribe of Saugus.

21. Page 23. The Indian name *Merrimack* is said to mean "Swift-Water-Place."

22. Page 23. Namaoskeag, now Amoskeag, was the traditional chief residence of Passaconnaway. See Potter's History of Manchester, N. H., p. 56. There are traditions that indicate that Passaconnaway may have had several temporary residences.

23. Page 24. This island is Sewall's, about three miles above the city proper of Concord.

24. Page 24. The location of the island is about a mile north of the mouth of the Souhegan.

25. Page 25. A thoughtful contemplation of Passaconnaway seems to suggest the idea that he was much more than a mere magician. A savage of extraordinary natural talents, and of keen practical intelligence, there are apparent indica-

tions that he excelled in that nobility of soul that seems at times to surmount the mere world of sense and for the time being dwell in the loftier realms of soulful realization.

26. Page 26. A fanciful meaning ascribed to the name *Winnipesaukee* is " The Smile of the Great Spirit."

27. Page 30. The Tarrantine tribe of Indians, foes of the Penacooks, lived east of the Penobscot River in Maine.

28. Page 30. The Mohog, or Mohawk, tribe of Indians, perennial enemies of the Penacooks, lived in the valley of the Mohawk River in New York.

29. Page 30. The early eminence called Sugar Ball, on the east side of the Merrimack River, and opposite the north end of the Main Street of the city of Concord.

30. Page 30. The spot is called Fort Eddy at the present time.

31. Page 32. See note 7.

32. Page 32. Pentucket, the same as Pawtucket, was in the vicinity of Lowell, Mass.

33. Page 32. Swampscot was in the vicinity of Exeter, N. H.

34. Page 32. Newichwannock, sometimes Newichewannock, was in the vicinity of Berwick Falls, Maine.

35. Page 32. The term *Bashaba* is said to be equivalent to Emperor. The tribes under Bashaba are affirmed to be as many as sixteen, representing a domain extending from Maine to Massachusetts. However, by referring to note 7,

the reader is reminded that a local name of a tribe does not always appear to imply a strictly natural classification of subordinate divisions of the Indian race.

36. Page 35. It is but natural to suppose that, before civilization occupied the soil of New Hampshire, and in consequence of civilized settlements elsewhere, Passaconnaway was duly informed of the incipient progress of a new order of things in America, which history asserts he at first feared.

37. Page 35. Reference is here made to the somewhat rare geographical fact that, between the Great Bay and the Atlantic Ocean, the Piscataqua River both flows and reflows to and from the sea, according to the alternate motion of the tides.

38. Page 36. History asserts that Passaconnaway was possibly first known to the English through Christopher Leavitt, who met the great chief at Piscataqua, when on a mission from Massachusetts, the year being 1623.

39. Page 36. Among the Indians, the rite of smoking the pipe together was emblematic of peace.

40. Page 38. The English trader thus slain, and whose murderer was delivered to civil authority by Passaconnaway, bore the name of Jenkins. The rendition was in 1632.

41. Page 40. The unfortunate and unjust treatment of Passaconnaway and his son and son's family here described occurred in 1642, result of a hasty act of the governor of Massachusetts.

42. Page 42. In 1644, Governor Winthrop, of Massachusetts, made the following assertion: " Passaconnaway and his

son *desire* to come under this government. He and one of his sons subscribe the articles; and *he* undertook for the others." Winthrop further recorded,—"Passaconnaway, the Merrimack sachem, came in and submitted to our government." See Bouton's History of Concord, N. H., p. 23.

43. Page 45. The annotated passage refers to the Rev. John Eliot, apostle to the Indians, of whom tradition says Passaconnaway entertained fear.

44. Page 47. Eliot on this occasion preached from the text found in Malachi I: 11, and tradition says he substituted " Gentiles " and " incense " by " Indians " and " prayer." The year was 1648.

45. Page 55. Tradition makes Passaconnaway, in this address, delivered in 1660, admit that he had vainly employed his magical arts against the English.

46. Page 58. It is not certainly known at what time Passaconnaway died, or at what age. He appears to have been living in 1663, and it is supposed that he died at the great age of about 120 years.

47. Page 59. This tract of land, including the two islands, is now embraced in the territory of Merrimack and Litchfield, New Hampshire towns. The islands are called Reed's.

48. Page 59. History attests the fact that the sons and successors of Passaconnaway measurably at least emulated his character.

49. Page 60. The medicine man, or conjuror, exercised his art to free others from the influence of evil spirits, doing so with noisy demonstrations.

NOTES TO THE LAST POWWOW.

———

1. Page 67. A spot within the limits of the city of Concord, N. H., in the valley of the Merrimack River, was the scene that prompted the theme of this narrative.

2. Page 68. A sachem, in the ordinary tribal relations of the Indians, appears to have been a chief of the first rank.

3. Page 68. Pehaungun is said to have been the last native Indian who died within the limits of Concord, where once roamed the Penacook tribe. Pehaungun's wigwam is said to have been on the present farm of Andrew Farnum, of East Concord.

4. Page 70. Passaconnaway was the first chief of Penacooks known to the white settlers of New Hampshire.

5. Page 70. See note 35 of THE SEER.

6. Page 70. See note 18 of THE SEER for the derivation of the name Passaconnaway.

7. Page 70. See note 6 of THE SEER.

8. Page 71. The executive skill, prudent counsel, and religious character of Passaconnaway are amply attested in history.

9. Page 74. Passaconnaway claimed that his spirit was in conscious communication with the Manit, or Manatou. See Note 10 of THE SEER.

10. Page 77. The Indian term *occuwee* was a name for spirituous liquor, or "fire-water."

11. Page 77. Tahanto is called a *sagamore*, a term which, strictly speaking, appears to have belonged to a chief of a rank lower than a *sachem*, though the terms are frequently interchanged by early historians. See note 2.

12. Page 77. On the 27th of October, 1668, Tahanto is said to have met a party of Englishmen who had come to Penacook (now Concord), and he advised them if they had any liquor to pour it out, as it would make the Indians "all one divill."

13. Page 78. Wonalancet emulated the virtues of his father with apparent strictness. He is said to have been converted by Eliot in 1674.

14. Page 78. Philip's Indian war broke out in 1675. As the intelligent reader knows, the white settlers of New England were not only thrown into great consternation, but many suffered in their lives or property, in consequence of it.

15. Page 79. Wonalancet retired into the wilderness as far as the head-waters of the Connecticut River. He was absent from civilized haunts a year. Returning, though subjected to suspicion and injury, he proved himself a sincere friend to the white man's cause.

16. Page 79. Cocheco is now the city of Dover, N. H.

17. Page 80. In 1676, Wonalancet, having submitted to English authority at Cocheco, saved the Widow Kimball and her five children, as the text asserts. The Kimball family was of Bradford, Mass.

18. Page 81. It is not certainly known how Wonalancet closed his earthly career. He appears to have joined the St. Francis tribe of Indians upon the border of Canada, and it is supposed he died among them.

19. Page 82. Kancamaugus was an able man, who attained some English education, being competent to write a passable letter, subscribing himself "John Hogkins," his colloquially assumed name. However, history asserts his unreliable character, and he is said to have been concerned in the Indian massacre at Cocheco, June 27, 1689.

20. Page 82. Major Waldron, commander of the English military station at Cocheco, previously to the massacre which cost him his life, had been warned of imminent danger from an Indian foray, but he disregarded the apprehension.

21. Page 82. At the time implied, there were wandering in New Hampshire a representation of Indians who had been engaged in Philip's war. These were considered somewhat as outlaws and were called "strange Indians."

22. Page 83. Major Waldron's assurance on this occasion was purely presumptive, as the sequel shows.

23. Page 83. Historic opinion has been divided in regard to the true judicial attitude in which Major Waldron stood to

8

the Indians. That he was an object of their vengeance is sure: that he deserved their revenge is not so certain. A number of Indians had been inveigled into captivity in consequence of their participation in Philip's war, and Waldron's fate sealed the natural resentment of the savages; but it is still claimed that the English act of betrayal was discountenanced by Waldron.

24. Page 83. History says the Indians rushed into Major Waldron's presence shouting, "Who shall judge Indians now?"

25. Page 84. It is said that not less than twenty-three persons were killed at this massacre.

26. Page 84. It appears that after the massacre at Cocheco a considerable number of the Penacook Indians repaired to the St. Francis tribe.

27. Page 85. Among these prospective settlers were Henry Rolfe and Richard Urann.

28. Page 86. See note 12 in reference to Penacook as the ancient name of Concord. See also note 7 of THE SEER.

29. Page 87. The Rev. Timothy Walker was the first minister of Concord, ordained and installed in 1730. His permanent home, made a garrison in 1729, is now the remodeled residence of the Hon. Joseph B. Walker, at the north end of Main Street.

30. Page 88. This son was afterwards Hon. Timothy Walker.

31. Page 89. Wattanummon lived in the vicinity of East

Concord. The stream by which Horseshoe Pond is drained into the Merrimack is called Wattanummon's Brook to this day. Wattanummon's wigwam stood near the south end of the railroad bridge across this brook.

32. Page 89. Ebenezer Eastman settled at Penacook as early as 1727, and built a block house on present land of John Frye, just south of the freight depot at East Concord. Eastman is said to have been the first settler in Penacook.

33. Page 89. The spot is now called Wattanummon's Field, being west of the Merrimack River and containing about 100 acres, owned by Hon. J. B. Walker, Hon. J. H. Pearson, and Charles Farnum.

34. Page 90. This chief was named Peorawarrah, and he is said to have lived below Penacook on the Merrimack River.

35. Page 90. This was Sewall's Island. See note 23 of THE SEER.

36. Page 91. The place where the body lodged is called Squaw Lot to this day. About eighty rods up the river from the bridge on the East Concord road is the spot where the body lodged, on land owned by Col. J. E. Pecker, the river having changed its course and left the spot inland.

37. Page 92. Pehaungun is supposed to have lived to the age of over 100 years.

38. Page 92. Pehaungun died about the year 1732.

39. Page 96. See note 17 of THE SEER for the definition of the Indian term *powwow*, which had both a personal and a collective application.

40. Page 97. The spot was probably not far from the site of the present capacious ice-house, where was once an elevation called Pond Hill, cut down when the Concord & Claremont Railroad traversed the spot.

41. Page 99. The time of the Last Powwow is not very definitely ascertained. It occurred between the years 1730 and 1744.

42. Page 102. In 1744, the War of the Austrian Succession broke out, involving the martial contention of the English and French, both in Europe and America. The outbreak of this war inaugurated a state of conflict between the English and French that lasted, with slight interruption, about twenty years. During this time, the English settlers of New England were in much peril of the incursions of Indians, who, from the borders of Canada, and in the interest of the French, swept southerly to prey upon the English, especially seeking captives to be held for pecuniary ransoms. Since a considerable portion of the Penacook tribe was dispersed among the St. Francis Indians, special enemies of the English, it is assumed that native Penacooks may have been engaged in some of the Indian forays from which the English settlers suffered during the time described.

www.ingramcontent.com/pod-product-compliance
Lightning Source LLC
Chambersburg PA
CBHW022141020726
47496CB00008B/2506